2001 PART 2: A VIRGIN'S ODYSSEY CONTINUES

KIMBERLEY KELLER

2001 Part 2: A Virgin's Odyssey Continues
Copyright: Kimberley Keller
Published: 2022

BASED ON A TRUE STORY

What evolved to become his choice,
Quickly became my chore,
But losing control of everything,
Led me closer to my own **freedom**.

CHAPTER 1

I tried desperately to find my thoughts and my breath as I sat parked outside my parents' bungalow with Gary.

"Aren't you grateful we're here?" he asked.

"Gary," I said finally, "how the fuck do you know where I live?"

He switched off the engine-

We couldn't stay here!

He turned to me. "Princess, I've warned you about your language."

How could he call me Princess here? This was my world. My real world. My life as a male. I'd neighbours. People who'd known me all my life. I wasn't Princess-

Gary lowered his window. "I need air."

He needed air!?! *I* needed privacy!

"I don't like bad language in normal, everyday occasions," he said.

What was normal or everyday about this?!?

"I accept it in sexual situations..."

I was frightened to death any one of my neighbours might hear him, never mind see him.

"I even encourage it, *sometimes*, in sexual situations-"

"Gary, stop. Put your window up, please. Turn the engine on. Let's get out of here."

"No."

My eyes were set dead ahead. "You *do* know where we are, don't you?"

"Yes."

"How? How can you know?"

"Baby..."

I cringed.

"You know the way I changed to a later flight?"

"Yes."

"I don't fly back until Saturday morning. I texted my wife, I told her I've to stay on for work. You've five more days with me."

Five more days!?! Saturday morning!?! My parents were coming back on Saturday morning!

"Just think how many times you can suck my cock-"

"Gary," I snapped. "Don't talk like that here. Your window's down. I live here. I don't want people to know."

"Okay, Princess."

I shushed him.

"Let's go inside," he said.

"What?"

"Let's go inside. Your neighbours can't see or hear you behind closed doors."

"Gary, that's my parents' house. I can't bring you in there."

"You're going to have to. I've nowhere else to stay." He opened the driver's door. "You coming?"

My insides felt like there were going to turn inside out.

"Come on... Princess."

I watched in awe as this man closed the car door behind him, then proceeded to walk up my parents' driveway and searched for the front door key on the set of keys in his hand.

He whistled.

I looked around myself in every direction, hoped no one was watching, then undid my seat belt and hurried after him.

Gary was already inside before I got to the front door.

I slammed it shut behind me, then locked it and ushered him into the kitchen where I immediately closed the blinds.

He stood in the centre of the room. "This is a lovely house, Princess."

Princess. I wondered did he know my real name as well.

"Hey, baby, cheer up, I know you want this too-"

"Gary, what the hell? You said you put your flight off until

Saturday, but that doesn't explain how you figured out where I lived? What's going on here, Gary?"

He could see I was shaking. "Relax," he insisted. "I'm not going to hurt you."

I couldn't relax.

"Stop trembling, baby."

I couldn't.

Gary sighed. "I thought you'd be happy, Princess."

I almost wanted to tell him to stop calling me that. "Just explain. Have you known who I am all along?"

"What?"

"Gary, how the hell do you know where I live?"

"Come here," he said, holding out his hands.

I shook my head, then backed away from him until I stepped so far as the oven.

"You remember I disappeared for an hour on Saturday?"

"Yes, Gary, how could I forget? You left me naked in the hotel room."

"I was here."

I froze.

"No, not literally *in* here. I was outside, Princess. I found your house."

I felt intruded. I felt invaded. I felt violated. "*How* did you find it, Gary? I want the truth."

"I'm still the same guy you wanted to give a blow job to-"

"Stop it," I snapped, holding my palm up. I couldn't begin to contemplate such thoughts right now. If anything, the thought of it made me sick to my stomach.

"I happened to look in your glove compartment."

What for, I wondered?

"I found documentation. It had this address registered to the vehicle. I decided to try to find where you lived. I asked a couple of people for directions. It was actually quite easy."

I was stunned.

"Princess, it wasn't supposed to shock you-"

"It has."

"This was supposed to be a surprise, something to cheer you up and hopefully make your week. Baby, I didn't even know I was going to change my flight until you offered to drive me to the airport. When I saw how upset you were about us parting, I just knew I had to make new arrangements. So I sprung this on you."

"I consider myself sprung, Gary." I put my head in my hands. "Shit, this is too weird-"

"Do you want me to go?" he asked.

"Go where? You said yourself you've nowhere to go."

Gary took a single step towards me. "So, I can stay?"

I let my hands slide to my cheekbones.

He took another step. "Here?"

"Gary..."

"With you?"

"My aunt Shauna's calling later."

"She doesn't have to see me, baby."

I shook my head. "You don't know my family, Gary. You really don't. She'll treat this place like it's more her home than mine. She'll nosy around every room."

He stood right in front of me. "We'll work it out, baby." He took my hands from my face. "I promise." He rubbed my hands in his. "Now, why don't you kiss me?"

CHAPTER 2

I hauled my hands out from within Gary's grasp and turned my face quickly from his. "No, Gary!"

Slats of light from between the blinds cast across my parents' kitchen.

"*That* can't happen here," I insisted, and slithered away from him.

Gary caught hold of my upper arm.

"Let go of me, Gary."

He easily turned me to him again, then grabbed hold of my other arm. "Why are you being like this, Princess?"

I almost felt my skin crawl at the sound of that word on his lips *here*. "This is not the right place for this. I can't be *her* here."

"Then be yourself, baby," he said.

"Don't call me that, Gary."

"I don't care if you're dressed up as a boy or a girl-"

"Don't tell me that. I can't hear that." I didn't want him to like me as a boy. Not ever.

Gary shook me. "Listen to me, you're overreacting. You're behaving like a child."

I stared defiantly into his eyes. "Let go of me, right this instant."

He ignored me.

"Gary."

He grinned. "You're sexy when you're angry."

"Stop it."

"Feisty," he added.

I tried in vain to pull away.

He laughed. "What're you going to do, Princess? Scream?"

I snarled.

"You're behaving like a child. Grow up. This is everything you could've dreamed of. You and I together, alone, for the next five days. In absolute privacy. We can do anything we want. We can do *everything* we want-"

"No, Gary, we can't!"

He breathed over me. "I'm so hard right now, Princess."

I ensured my eyes remained focused on his.

"Suck me," he whispered.

I shook my head.

"Right here, right now, in your parents' kitchen."

I felt like I was going to wretch.

"You remember what I said about you being supposed to do whatever I tell you without question?"

My nostrils flared.

"If I release your arms, you're not to turn away from me. You're not to run. In fact, you're not to move away at all, Princess... Understood?"

I said nothing.

He dug his fingers through my sweater into my flesh.

"You're hurting me, Gary," I whined, resorting to my more forced, feminine voice.

"No, I'm not."

But he was.

"You're going to obey me, Princess. Right?"

I raised my hands to his elbows, glimpsing my chipped red fingernails, and tried to take hold of him.

Gary tightened his hold. "Answer me," he snapped.

I gently touched his elbows. "Gary..." I caressed him. "I've nowhere to run to."

He hesitated, then he smiled. "Good girl."

I breathed a sigh of relief as he released me.

"I knew you'd see sense. We're here, Princess. This is our house for the week. Me, the man. And you, the woman. The lady. The-"

I swivelled on my athletic shoes and charged out of the

kitchen.

"Princess!" he yelled. "Come back here!"

I ran into the hall.

"Stop!"

I darted from the direction of the front door, instead opting to rush towards the bedrooms.

Gary charged after me.

I ran past my parents' bedroom, into my own and slammed the door behind-

Gary stuck his foot in the doorway, blocking me from shutting the door.

I pushed it pathetically against him. "Go away, Gary!"

He pushed back against me. "What're you doing?" he demanded.

"I don't want you in here."

"Why not, Princess?"

My heart was pounding. "Because..." It was a boy's bedroom.

"Baby?"

I couldn't answer him. I couldn't fight. I peeled my hands from the door.

He didn't push his way in.

I waited in the relative darkness, my curtains still drawn since Saturday.

He said nothing.

"Gary?" I asked.

He didn't answer.

I looked down.

His shoe wasn't there anymore.

"Gary?"

"I'm in your parents' bedroom," he said aloud.

Oh. My. God.

"Did *they* leave the door open?"

They did not.

"Or did you forget to close it when you were borrowing your mother's underwear and jewellery?"

Shame shackled my face in the most rouge of colours.

Gary elicited a forced, brief laugh.

"What?" I asked.

"Do you know what's going to happen in this bedroom of theirs, Princess? In this very bed? I'm going to fuck their daughter in it."

I gasped.

"I'm going to *take* your virginity."

I wasn't ready! I was still extremely sensitive from the brutal fucking my asshole took from the cucumber only yesterday.

The floorboards of my parents' bedroom creaked as Gary stepped around the room. "You'll never feel like a boy in this room again, Princess. I swear to you, I'll see to that."

I felt blood rush to my clit.

"I'm going to have orgasm after orgasm while I'm inside you on this bed."

I heard my breathing ragged.

Gary opened the door to my bedroom and switched on the light.

I tried not to cower before him.

"You disobeyed me," he said, his eyes inspecting every corner of the room and ignoring me. "You ran away. That's not good, Princess. Not good at all."

I hesitated.

His eyes roamed the compact discs which gave away anything but a feminine taste.

"I'm out of my comfort zone, Gary, I'm sorry."

He tutted.

"Just please bear with me. This room, it isn't *me*. It isn't where Princess belongs. I can't be my true self around you here. This whole house feels wrong."

He stared at my desktop computer. "This is where you masturbate when you read my e-mails," he said.

I felt so embarrassed.

"And this chair. This is where you sit with your jeans at your ankles, your little clitty in your hand, tugging away."

"Gary, please don't-"

"Drop your jeans to your ankles, right now, Princess," he said firmly.

I undid the top button, then the three at the fly.

Gary didn't even look at me to check.

I let my jeans fall.

He rested his hand on the back of my chair, as he looked down.

I knew what he was looking for.

"All that she-cream you spilled for me here... Set your clit out over the top of your panties."

I obliged. I couldn't fight him anymore. My resilience was worn out. I was a mismatch of defeat and diligence, ostracised so far from my resistance.

"It won't work, y'know," he said.

"What, Gary?"

"You're trying to play me, Princess."

What?

"You think by instantaneously obeying me now I'll forget that stunt you just pulled in the kitchen. I *won't*, Princess. And you're going to be punished."

I shook my head. "Gary, I'm being genuine-"

"You're *not* being genuine. You're being a spoilt, little brat. You've been my electronic whore in here a hundred times or more..."

My jaw dropped in shock.

"... And you're not going to fool me by pretending you can't be a real whore in this room right now, Princess."

I was stunned into silence.

Gary looked at me for the first time since he'd entered the room. "Get on your knees."

I hesitated, then swallowed saliva.

He unzipped his fly and pulled out his mammoth cock.

I followed the fist he made around it. "Gary, I..."

"If you don't drop to your knees by the time I've counted to five, I might as well just force you face down on this bed... And, by God, if that happens, Princess, nothing will stop me from fucking your brains out."

I froze, gobsmacked, unable to believe the words he was using to me.

"One."

I was trembling. Shaking.

"Two."

I couldn't believe this man was threatening to-

"Three."

Actually.

"Four."

Make me.

He growled.

Against my will?

"Five," he said finally.

My eyes blazed wide with fear.

Gary grabbed my clit with one hand, tugging me towards him, and sent his free arm slamming into my back, shoving me to the bed.

My knees crashed onto the mattress first. "Gary!" My palms second.

He leapt on top of me, pinning me down with his weight.

I screamed.

Gary slapped his palm across my mouth, silencing me, then yanked my thong to one side.

I felt his thick cock between my buttocks, right up against my hole.

He snarled.

I was powerless to fight him off.

"You're supposed to obey me without question, Princess."

My saliva spilled through his fingers as I pitifully tried to protest.

"Now you know the punishment must happen."

I shook my head so vehemently I freed my lips from him palm. "No, no!"

"All you'd to do was suck my cock, like you promised," he said, his mouth to my ear as he ground his cock against my virgin ass.

I was panting, squirming. "This can't happen here, Gary."

"Why not?"

"Because in here my name's not Princess... It's-"

"Mark!" called a female voice from down the hall.

All colour drained from my face. "Aunt Shauna," I whispered.

CHAPTER 3

"She's here," I said almost silently, as precum from Gary's gargantuan head leaked onto my opening.

He actually thrust himself against it.

"Mark?" Aunt Shauna called again. "Where are you, dear?"

I felt sheer terror as a floorboard creaked under her movement.

She was coming up the hall.

Gary eased his weight off me.

"Just a second," I called, sliding out from under him to the floor and dragging my jeans back up.

"You're awake?" she said.

"Barely."

She seemed a little taken aback as I appeared in the doorway of my bedroom.

I strutted forward, shoving my fingernails into my pockets.

"Mark?"

I was shaking. I was dishevelled. My jeans weren't fitting right. My sweater wasn't sitting right. And my whole demeanour reeked of shame and guilt.

"What's wrong?"

I shook my head.

"Mark, *tell me.*" She tried to look over my shoulder.

Gary was silent on my bed.

I wondered if his cock was still out. Oh fuck, if Aunt Shauna found him my entire life was finished.

"What is it?"

"Nothing," I lied. Nothing other than the fact Gary was in my house and he'd just threatened to fuck me.

"You look awful, Mark."

I hated how he now knew my name. My real name. This wasn't supposed to be.

Aunt Shauna physically stopped me in the hall. "You're going to tell me exactly what's going on here." She looked me up and down. "Something's wrong, isn't it?"

I wondered how she could tell. Could she smell him on me? Could she still smell my perfume? My cum? His?

"Mark?"

I could still feel the residual sensation of his mammoth cock right up against my hole. How powerless I'd been to prevent him taking me further. Staking me further. Fucking me right there and then on my bed.

Aunt Shauna breathed heavily over me, then cast her eyes to the bedroom. Something changed in her eyes.

My bed creaked.

"Would you like a cup of tea, Aunt Shauna?" I said, my voice a bundle of nerves.

She stared past me. "Mark, is someone else here?"

I couldn't answer.

"Just tell me, if there is."

I was so afraid of him.

"Say the word, and we'll go."

What if he hurt her too?

"We can go together."

I balled my hands into fists in my pockets.

"We'll be safe if we get out of here now, together."

And I wouldn't be forced to have sex with him. I tried to ignore the disappointment which deployed in my bowels.

There were heavy footsteps in my bedroom.

Aunt Shauna's eyes widened in unison with mine.

But she wasn't watching mine.

"Who-"

"Hello there," Gary said, his accent so drastically different to ours. "You must be Aunt Shauna?"

I thought I was going to faint.

Aunt Shauna stuttered a series of meaningless consonants and vowels.

"I'm Gary," he said, and almost barged me out of the way as he reached his hand out to my aunt.

She reluctantly took it.

My eyes darted to his crotch.

His fly was up. His shaft sheathed in his clothing.

Aunt Shauna's eyes went from mine. To his. Then to his groin. She'd seen me look.

I gulped as my face reddened.

"Gary?" she asked, shaking his hand and looking to me again for reassurance.

"Yes," I said, with no logical reason forthcoming.

"And who the hell are you, Gary?"

Oh God. This was going to get worse. A lot worse.

"Me?" he said, laughing.

I swallowed.

"Aren't you going to introduce me, Pr-"

"Mark," I interrupted, hating myself all over again.

Aunt Shauna snatched her hand away from him. "What were you doing in my nephew's bedroom?"

My jaw dropped.

"What the hell are you even doing in my sister's home?"

Gary stood, composed and confident, but suspiciously – no, guiltily – silent.

"*Who* the hell are you, Gary?"

He laughed. "My apologies, I have you at a disadvantage."

"You most certainly do, sir."

"I'm Gary."

"We've established that," she said. "But who the fuck are you Gary?"

I'd not heard my aunt use that word before, and sensed the disgust from Gary.

"The boy didn't want me to say anything," he began, making me cringe, "but you know what they're like at that age, hormones racing and all that. He was up in the middle of the night, on his computer. Sorry, Mark, I don't wish to embarrass you."

I was beyond that.

"Let's just say he got carried away with some of the websites he was looking at. Nothing too bad, mind. Just a little red-blooded, let's say."

Aunt Shauna shot me a look of disapproval.

"As so many young people do. I've had a look at the site, it's nothing to be concerned about. However, it seems he accidentally downloaded a virus and the computer crashed. He was in a panic when it wouldn't restart. His parents are away and he was afraid they'd be angry with him for what he'd done."

"Uh-huh."

"I got an early wake-up call this morning to see if I could come over and have a look at the computer..."

Aunt Shauna pushed past me and headed to my room.

"So here I am."

Aunt Shauna stopped in the middle of my bedroom floor. "But the computer isn't even on." She looked to the drawn curtains at the window. "Have you even started to look at it?" She turned to face us, stood together.

Gary hesitated.

"Yes," I said. "He fixed it. It's fine."

Aunt Shauna looked at the bed. "Then why were you both still in here?"

"I'd *just* finished fixing it," Gary insisted, then walked into the room. "Let's give her a little test." He pushed the on button on my desktop.

Aunt Shauna waited.

I, too, with baited breath.

The desktop fan kicked in.

"He really was terrified of his parents finding out, Shauna."

"Porn?" Aunt Shauna snapped. "You should be ashamed of yourself, Mark."

"I am," I said, looking down at my sensible shoes. "Please don't tell my mother and father."

The desktop continued to boot up as normal.

"I know nothing about computers," Aunt Shauna said, looking Gary over.

"Really?" he asked. "Oh, there's nothing much to them when you know how."

She smiled.

"I'm pretty much self-taught, Shauna."

"Is that so, Gary?" She was *really* looking at him.

I'd no idea if he'd any real idea about computers, or if he was just bullshitting. "Everything seems to be working fine now," I said, before the Windows icon had even appeared.

Aunt Shauna shushed me. "Quiet, the adults are having a conversation."

I felt my thong chafe at my rear.

"*Is* it fixed, Gary?"

"Seems to be."

"My nephew's hero," she said.

Gary forced a chuckle. "You won't say anything to Mark's parents, will you?"

She hesitated.

"Please, aunt Shauna."

She exhaled. "Okay, I'll keep quiet about it..." She looked to Gary. "Now you're *my* hero too." She gestured back down the hall. "Say, Gary, I didn't see another car parked outside, do you need a lift anywhere?"

"Oh dear," Gary said, hunching over the computer as the password prompt appeared on the screen.

Aunt Shauna leaned alongside him.

Too close for my liking.

"What is it?" she asked, looking right in his eyes.

He returned her gaze. "I'm going to have to take a rain check on that lift, Shauna, I'm afraid."

"You are?"

I looked at the bed. Why didn't I feel fear that he was trying to stay?

"Yeah, this thing's not as fixed as I thought. I'm going to have to do a full system reinstall."

"A full system what?" she asked.

"It'll take a couple of hours."

Aunt Shauna hesitated.

I was just waiting for her to tell me to put the kettle on-

"I can't stay that long," she said. "I've a date with the high street shops, and I don't intend on keeping them waiting." She looked at me again finally. She stared.

Had she noticed how many adjustments I'd made to my jeans and sweater? How much effort I'd put into concealing my bra? Any hint of my thong panties? And my stockings between the end of my jeans and the beginning of my shoes?

"See me out, Mark," she barked. "Gary, lovely to meet you. I hope I see you again sometime."

"Yes, Shauna, you too." He drummed his fingers on the keyboard, making it look important.

I headed down the hall, hoping she'd quickly follow.

"The kitchen," she said. "Go to the kitchen, Mark."

Of course, I thought, she'd let herself in that way with her spare key. I'd have to remember to lock it behind her, and leave my key in the door so she couldn't force her way back in again... Unless Gary was fucking me against my will, and I needed saving. Oh fuck, what was he going to do to me when she left?

"Mark," she said, quietly closing the kitchen door to the hall behind her.

"Yes, Aunt Shauna?"

She slapped me across the face.

What the fuck? I almost pulled my hand out of my pocket to shield myself from another.

"That's for being a disgusting, little pervert. How dare you get up to such sordid activities while my sister's away on her first proper holiday without you!"

If she only knew.

"You listen to me, young man, and you listen good. I've a good mind to tell her what you've been up to. A mother has a right to know she's raised a pervert." Aunt Shauna stared me

down, then glanced to my hands stuffed in my pockets.

Oh God, if she demanded I get them out-

"But I won't ruin her holiday, understand me? You owe me for this, Mark. *Big* style."

"Yes, Aunt Shauna."

"I mean it."

"Yes, Aunt Shauna."

"And I do intend on collecting on that."

I wanted to usher her to the back door. "Yes, Aunt Shauna."

She finally made her way across the floor and set her palm on the handle. She froze.

I felt panic rise inside.

"One more thing, dear..."

Dear was... Good? It was certainly better than disgusting, little pervert.

"Open your bedroom curtains for Gary, okay? You might want to live like a hermit in the dark all day, but that gentleman is trying to do a day's work... Treat him right."

"I will, Aunt Shauna."

She opened the back door. "Oh, I forgot to ask, how do you know him?"

"Uh..." My mind went blank.

"Is he single?"

I shook my head. He was mine!

"Married?"

I reluctantly nodded. He wasn't mine.

Aunt Shauna scrunched up her face. "All the good one's are."

CHAPTER 4

"Gary," I started, walking up the hall towards my room, "we need to set some ground rules." Some boundaries.

He was sat in my computer chair, facing the door, legs spread and naked.

"Jesus, Gary, put your clothes on."

"Your aunt's away?"

"Yes, but that's not the point. We can't be like that here. It isn't right." I glanced at my male shoes and clothes folded in the corner.

He took hold of his erection. "I disagree."

I watched as he slowly masturbated before me.

"I'm wanking in your bedroom, baby."

I couldn't keep my eyes off it.

"You know how to make me stop?"

"How?" I asked, gazing at the bulbous head.

"Suck it, Princess."

I exhaled.

"You promised you would."

"Gary, I just don't feel comfortable committing any sexual acts under this roof."

He picked up his pace and grunted. "I do, baby."

I could feel my legs weaken. I wanted his throbbing cock in my mouth. I did. I really did. Just not here in my own bedroom, surrounded by every reminder of my birth gender.

"Why don't you take off your clothes, Princess?"

"No," I said, but part of me wanted to be persuaded.

"Just your clothes, not your underwear. You do look so good in your lingerie."

I nodded, then pulled my sweater over my head and threw it to the floor.

Gary swapped his shaft from one palm to the other. "Good girl, you know it makes sense."

"I still want to talk to you." I unbuttoned my jeans. "About what happened before Aunt Shauna walked in. I'm not happy about it, Gary. That was not cool."

He said nothing as he stared at the lace front of my panties.

I stepped out of my jeans and fixed my stockings into place.

"Give me a twirl."

I turned my rear to him.

He thudded his fist faster.

I didn't want to use the R word. It was too extreme. "Please never do anything to me, against my will." I pulled my thong higher on my hips and leaned myself ever so slightly forward to accentuate my ass.

"Beautiful," he said.

I ran my hands through my hair.

"Why don't you go fix your hair and make-up, Princess, see if you feel more *at home* when you become your true self?"

I half-looked over my shoulder.

He was pulling himself off so good.

"Okay," I whispered. "Just don't cum... Not without me here to catch it."

"And where are you going to catch it, Princess?"

I began to strut sexily out of the room. "In my mouth, of course, lover."

CHAPTER 5

I applied my make-up in the bathroom, the door locked to ensure my privacy. How did Gary have such a hold over me? Such an influence against my wishes in favour of his own?

I looked good, and smiled at my reflection. Okay, so it wasn't *entirely* against my wishes to be getting into my make-up again. But being in this house was very much not my idea. How the hell was I supposed to keep him here, safely, until Saturday morning? Especially not with my Aunt Shauna now on look-out.

I retouched my fingernails.

Gary audibly grunted in my bedroom.

I didn't want him to cum without me, but perhaps it was for the best. Maybe then I could get him to have the conversation.

The floorboards creaked in the hall.

Gary knocked the bathroom door.

"Did you cum?" I demanded.

"No," he said, croakily. "I stopped myself just in time..."

"What is it, Gary?"

"I inhaled your pillow."

I gulped.

"Then your duvet. And finally your sheets."

I sprayed myself with my mother's perfume as my face reddened. "Yes?"

"I know your natural scent from you lay in my arms, Princess. It's so beautiful. I know you're only a door away from me, but... I miss you."

I wasn't sure if he was joking.

"Do you miss me?"

I hesitated. "Yes, Gary."

He was silent.

I did like him. But at times he was very overbearing, and the result very overwhelming.

"I'll wait for you in your room," he said, and the floorboards creaked again as he returned.

I tied my hair seductively up. I loved how it exposed my bare neck and shoulders, and hoped he'd kiss me again in those favourite spots of mine he'd found.

My make-up was flawless, my nails perfect and I just loved how I felt in my bra, thong and stockings.

Only one thing remained.

I unlocked the bathroom door, then crossed the hall to my parents' bedroom. I picked out a pair of her stilettos, slipped my feet into them and took a practice walk around the room until I felt confident.

I made my way to my own room, then stopped in the doorway.

Gary was laid back naked on my bed, his legs spread, his hands by his side and his cock, semi-erect, lying sexily across one thigh.

"I'm not going to tell you to do anything, Princess," he said.

Good, I thought. Perhaps I could even start to relax in my own house and maybe find a way to enjoy having him here. But I had to check. "*Ever* again?" I asked.

He raised one eyebrow. "For now, baby."

I decided to let it go. For now.

Gary stared at me. "You look amazing."

"Thank you." I rubbed the front of my thong. "You look very hot yourself, lover."

"I love it when you call me that, Princess."

I shuddered as I recalled the feel of his cock between my buttocks less than an hour ago, and how fearful I'd felt.

"Where are you right now?" he asked.

"Right here," I lied, and crawled onto the end of my bed. I ran my hands over his legs, sensually touching his shins, then his calves and knees. I kissed his thighs, starting with the bare one, then switching sides, laying my lips across every part of his skin except where his cock lay. It looked so good. I breathed over it.

He twitched.

I breathed again, and watched in awe as his skin tingled.

"That feels amazing, Princess. It's teasing, yet pleasing."

I gently ran my fingernails over his testicles, caressing both his pubic hair and his scrotum.

His eyes locked on mine.

I lowered my face to his crotch. "I can't believe I'm going to do this here, Gary."

"It's okay, baby, you can do it..."

I breathed deeply in.

"But only if you want to."

I took hold of his cock in one hand, pulled back his foreskin and slipped my lips against his slit, kissing it gently.

"Baby," he whispered.

I slid my tongue under his slit, then deliberately dragged his foreskin forward with my fingers, sheathing the tip of my tongue.

"Wow."

I massaged his balls with my other hand, hauled back his foreskin and swished my tongue around the circumference of his head.

His shaft was growing.

I could see it. I fed more of it between my lips until I could feel it. Yes, I finally had his cock in my mouth! Oh my God, it felt so good. I could lose myself on it. Almost forget where I was. I grabbed hold of his balls.

Gary winced. "Careful, baby."

I relaxed my grip. A little. But I my desires for his cock were deepening. I moved my mouth more than half-way down his member, until I was forced to release it from my palm and take it deeper.

"Oh, Princess, this is incredible."

I stuffed my own hand in my panties.

He grunted.

I wondered how long he'd last as I funnelled his phallus further towards the back of my throat.

"*You're* incredible," he said.

I gagged, just a little, but it was enough to force me to momentarily release him. I sucked in a little air, then I sucked him back inside me.

Gary reached his fingers down so he could lovingly caress my hair.

I sensually licked around his shaft in swift, energetic motions. Then I sucked him up and down. I couldn't help myself within my own underwear, tugging on my tiny clit.

"You can take them off, if it'd make you more comfortable, baby."

I slipped my thong down to below my knees, then twisted my body to one side to make it easier to masturbate.

Gary's cock hit the roof of my mouth.

I gargled it down towards my throat again.

My mobile, in my jeans on the floor, received a text message.

I momentarily looked away from Gary's crotch.

He gently turned me back to his cock.

I swallowed him to his base, making sure I ignored the instinct to gag.

His eyes rolled back in his head.

I could feel his balls in my palm, hungry and bloated. I was determined I was going to catch some – if not all – of his hot cum in my mouth.

"I'm getting close," he groaned.

I greedily made love to his member with my mouth. This felt so good. So right. Like I was literally born to be in this position on a man. I temporarily realised my surroundings and hesitated.

Gary opened his eyes again.

I winked at him, then stuffed my lips with so much of him I was certain he could no longer see anything of his cock beneath his pubes.

He held me in place for a number of seconds.

Somehow, I didn't feel threatened.

He released me the moment I retreated.

I quickly gasped for air, then took him down again.

"You're perfect, Princess... I wish I could last longer."

I was so flattered I almost didn't realise my own pleasure, as suddenly my clitty dribbled precum onto my duvet.

He smiled down. "Baby, if you can time it so we cum at the same time... That'd be something else." He stroked my face. "But no pressure. What you're doing is amazing."

But I *did* feel pressure, although I welcomed it and set about reaching my own orgasm, tightening my legs together so I could rub my stockings against each other. The feel of the nylon was such a turn-on. As was Gary's gargantuan shaft in my mouth. I sucked harder than before on it, as if I wanted to drain his sperm into my mouth. I imagined how warm it'd feel. How gooey. How oh so dreamy.

He jolted under me.

I calmly steadied him, glancing up as I reassured him with a meaningful suck to his base.

He smiled so sexily back down to me.

I hammered at my own sex, determined to climax.

"I don't wanna hold back any longer," he whispered. "I can't."

I eagerly devoured him. I furiously fisted my she-phallus. I could feel his cock throb on my tongue. My own began to vibrate differently. It was happening. We were teetering on the brink of orgasm together.

Gary's stomach muscles tensed.

Mine did so in unison.

I switched my fingers from his balls to the base of his shaft, gripping it tightly and trying to milk it into my mouth.

Gary erupted his sperm.

I was instantaneously propelled backwards by my instinct, but I clamped my lips on the head of his member.

He volleyed more between my lips.

I creamed onto my thighs and stocking tops, eagerly pumping away. I felt more of his hot, juicy cum land on my tongue.

Gary was grunting wildly.

I hoped he'd witnessed me cum too. I leaked yet more, feeling such pride, as I finally released my clitty. My mouth was filling up more than I was prepared to take. I quickly reached up and unhooked my bra, freeing it from my body.

Gary's cock slipped free from my lips.

I couldn't swallow. And I couldn't hold it any longer. I sat up and let his spunk drool from the corners of my mouth, down my face to my chin and then it fell to my chest in huge, long globs.

He wheezed as he took hold of his cock, squeezing out the last of his orgasm. "You came too, Princess!"

I opened my mouth, and let an insurmountable load of his cum fall from my lips. It dripped to my chest, my stomach and even above my clit. "I did, lover." I gathered up some of his goo, then rubbed it into my sex. "Oh, Gary, that feels so good."

"Allow me," he said, then leaned forward, collecting some of my cum from my stockings, and pressed it into the foreskin of my sex. "Now we're one, our love juices entwined together on her." He sensually rubbed my clitty.

I could still taste some of his sperm on my tongue.

"Come here, Princess."

I was surprised, albeit pleasantly, when he kissed me, swapping both saliva and his cum on our tongues. I kissed him more intently, and accidentally smeared our cum on his skin when I caressed his face and his shoulders without thought.

Gary didn't seem to notice – or care – and passionately kissed me, massaging my tongue and sucking his own sperm from my mouth.

I was breathless when we finally broke. "My God, Gary, I didn't expect that." I was fanning myself with my palm. "I'm light-headed."

"I'm so happy, Princess." He looked down, collected more of my meagre amount of cum and rubbed it into his foreskin. "We're covered in each other's orgasms." He looked to my mouth. "I'd like to see you swallow sometime."

I giggled. "We'll see."

He caught my hand in his. "Did I say I was asking, Princess?"

I knew that tone. I saw that look in his eye. I couldn't let this go unchallenged any longer.

CHAPTER 6

Gary grinned as he let of go of my hand and rose from the bed. "You should check your mobile. I'm sure I heard a text come in."

But wait! We needed to chat-

"Let me see what your bathroom has," he continued, walking out of my room.

I noticed some sperm had spilled on my duvet. I wasn't sure whose was whose. I slid off the bed and onto my knees.

"You've no shower, Princess. Okay, I can live with that..."

I crawled over to my jeans on the floor.

"So long as you agree to bath with me."

I doubted I'd have a choice in the matter anyway. "I'd like that, Gary," I said. "Could you switch the emersion on? It's just outside the bathroom. It's the only way we'll get hot water at this time of year."

Gary whistled. "Ah, yes, summer. The perfect time of year to spend with you, baby. This way we've no excuse to waste much time with clothes."

I fished out my phone.

Gary walked back into my room. "I plan on spending most of this week naked, do you?"

MY MOTHER – Why is there a strange man in my house?

"Aunt Shauna, for fu- goodness sake."

"What's she say, Princess?"

"It's not her. It's my mother." I looked up to him. "She knows about you."

Gary grinned.

"This isn't funny, Gary."

He laughed. "I think it is. Aunt Shauna's your mother's sister, right?"

I nodded.

"She was dying to tell your mother about me. Couldn't you tell?" He stood so confidently – and handsomely – naked, his cock still thick and prominent, despite his erection subsiding. "She fancied me."

"No, she-"

My mobile beeped again.

MY MOTHER – Will you bloody answer me when I text you!?!

"Sorry, Gary, I-"

"Do what you've got to do," he said, and turned his back to me. "You'll learn the hard way, Princess... I'm guessing you always do."

I started to type out my reply.

Gary began to go through my CD collection.

ME – Mother I didn't think Aunt Shauna was going to tell you until you got home. I accidentally downloaded a virus. I needed someone to fix my computer. Sorry x

"I hope you're not apologising to her," Gary said.

I stared at his magnificent rear. It really was something else. His buttocks were so prominent. I hadn't really considered if I had a thing for men's asses, but I knew next time I sucked him off I wanted to be on my knees, clinging onto those buttocks, dragging my fingers through his flesh-

MY MOTHER – What are you talking about? I haven't spoken to your Aunt Shauna. She told me she'd be calling to see you tonight. I called the neighbours to check on you. Why are you bringing men into our home?

"Oh God," I said aloud.

"I'm sure it's nothing, Princess."

I looked up to him. "She knows you're here, but it wasn't

Aunt Shauna who told her. She says she called the neighbours to check on me... She wants to know why I'm bringing men into her home."

He laughed. "*Men.*"

"Gary, this is serious!"

He half-turned to look at me. "It isn't."

I slightly cowered, such was the disdain he had for me in his glance.

"Either the two of you have got your wires crossed, which you have, or..."

I clutched my mobile tight in my trembling fingers. "Or what, Gary?"

"Or she already knows the truth about you. Why else would she insinuate something insidious?"

"She couldn't," I insisted.

"Don't be so sure, Princess. Look at you, you're beautiful. You're so naturally feminine. You were born to be a girl."

"I hide it from her, Gary. I hide it so well."

He turned around completely to face me. "Look at you, baby, you can't help yourself. Your eyes go straight for my dick. You're naturally drawn to it. I bet you've been the same way for years."

"What?" I asked.

"I bet every time a man walks into a room, your eyes are instantly drawn to his crotch. Your mother's bound to have noticed. She knows what you're like. Even better than I do."

I was speechless. He was making me sound like some rampant slut!

"C'mon, baby, it's nothing to be ashamed of. You look at my cock right now and tell me what you want to do with it-"

"Gary, I-"

"Don't dismiss it. Look. Tell me the truth."

I dared glance at his girth. A glance turned into a stare. It was seconds before I realised I was open-mouthed. "I... I want to suck on it again."

"Good girl," he said, and slid his cock into my mouth again.

I couldn't help myself and surrendered to my whims, sucking

on his member once more. I knew I'd a text to reply to. Urgently. To dispel any hint of my sexuality she had in her head.

"She probably has every idea what you're doing right now, Princess."

I tried to look up.

"A mother knows."

I hesitated in my sucking.

Gary drove his stiffening cock deeper. "Being a good, little cocksucker is nothing to be ashamed of, Princess. Your mother should be proud of you."

My nostrils flared as I engulfed my lips on him.

"You're a wonderful daughter."

I sucked him to his base, nuzzling my nose in the warm, familiar scent of his pubes.

"A wonderful, cock-sucking daughter."

Why were such phrases turning me on so much? I should've been ashamed. Abhorred. Even to the point where I wrestled my mouth from his cock. But I couldn't. I was hooked. Both on his flesh and on the way he described me.

"She'd probably be relieved it's only one man you're servicing in here..."

My man.

"And not the dozens in her worst suspicions about you."

Oh my God. I momentarily imagined myself giving oral sex to man after man in this bedroom today. It was terrible! Terribly incredible!

Gary tried to pull his cock out from my mouth.

I was so brazen as I dragged my lips over it. I flung my fingernails around to his ass and hauled him so close his balls banged off my chin.

"She knows what you're doing, Princess," he said.

I mumbled into his cock.

"She knows you're sucking my cock right this moment."

I mumbled my agreement.

"Your mother knows what you are."

I was addicted to it.

"What are you, Princess?"

I looked up, my face full of cock, emphasising exactly what I was, when my mobile suddenly started to ring.

CHAPTER 7

"Don't answer that," he barked.

I had to!

"I mean it, Princess, let her work out for herself you're not her little girl anymore…"

What? She didn't even know I was-

"You're *my* little girl now."

The time for fooling around was over. I released his rod from my mouth, leaving a trail of saliva between his slit and my lips – I had to. I looked at my mobile. "It's her, Gary. I have to answer this, or she'll have half the neighbourhood at the front door. Surely neither of us wants that."

He sighed. "Okay."

I grabbed my phone and headed out to the hall. "Hello?" I said, ignoring the sight of my clitty swinging to and fro above my stocking tops.

"Mark, what on earth is going on back there?" my mother demanded. "Who are these men you're bringing into our house? What are you doing with them? Answer me at once!"

"Mother, you've got it all wrong. You're confused."

Gary appeared behind me.

I kept walking, and opened the door to the living room.

"*I've* got it all wrong? Excuse me, dear, Betty next door said she saw you get out of our car with a strange man."

I wondered if Betty also reported that he'd been driving my parents' car. If she had, I was done for. "He's not a strange man," I insisted, standing in the middle of the room.

"Excuse me? Betty said she'd never seen him before. And she described him! He doesn't sound like anyone we know!"

Gary followed me into the living room, shutting the door behind him. His cock was still so hard. "What are you?" he mouthed to me.

"He's a computer repairman," I said, sounding so embarrassed to say that in front of him.

Gary began to walk around me.

"I downloaded a virus. It was an accident."

Gary felt my rear.

"I didn't realise what I was downloading, mother."

He walked in front of me.

"Oh my God," my mother shrieked. "I can only begin to imagine what horrors you thought you were downloading. What have I told you about that internet? You shouldn't be on it, unsupervised. You need to stay away from so much. I hope the police aren't going to need to get involved."

"What? Mother, no–"

"What are you?" Gary mouthed, holding his member out to me.

I could barely concentrate with that thing in front of me. I was mesmerised by it.

Gary continued to circle me.

"Mark, who on earth is this repairman? Is he someone you know?"

He swatted my behind.

"Kind of," I said.

"I'm very suspicious, dear. I don't like you getting into cars with strange men, especially *our* car."

"I didn't. I–"

"Betty saw you together. Betty sees everything. You know what she's like. I'm going to have all the neighbours watching the house likes hawks now. Just you wait and see."

I was relieved the blinds were already drawn on every window.

"What are you?" Gary mouthed again.

"A cocksucker," I mouthed back.

"Excuse me?" mother asked. "I thought you said something."

"What? No."

"I heard you say something under your breath, Mark."

Gary reached between my legs and started to fondle my sex.

I steeled my teeth to suppress my pleasure in silence.

"Are you listening to me?" mother demanded.

He touched me so good down there. I loved that about him. He could make my clitty feel so good.

"Mark?"

"Say it again," Gary mouthed.

"A cocksucker," I mouthed back. "Your cocksucker."

"Is something wrong with this line?" mother asked.

Gary gestured to his cock. "Show me," he mouthed. "Right now."

"Nothing's wrong with it, mother," I said.

"I'm angry with your Aunt Shauna as well."

I took myself down to one knee.

"She should've told me there was a strange man in the house."

I dropped to both knees.

"And how was it you intended to pay this so-called repairman?"

I opened my mouth.

"Well?"

Gary slipped his dick between my lips.

"Mark?"

I sucked on a cock while my mother's voice rang in my ear.

"Answer me right now," she said.

Gary groaned.

"What is that noise?"

I let him slip out from my mouth. "With the money on the mantelpiece," I said. "I'll pay him with that, mother."

Gary turned to the mantelpiece.

"Hang on, Mark, you'll *pay* him?"

"That's what I said, of course."

Gary looked behind the clock on the mantelpiece.

Mother hesitated.

I didn't like it when mother hesitated.

"Mark, I need to ask you a question and I want you to tell me the absolute truth..."

I gulped. "Okay."

Gary approached me again.

"This so-called repairman, is he still there?"

I froze.

"I'd like to speak to him."

I almost dropped the phone.

"I'm not asking, dear. Go and get him. I know what you're like. You don't enjoy speaking in front of other people on the phone. So I'll give you a minute to go get him."

I was distraught.

"What?" Gary mouthed.

I placed my palm over the speaker. "She wants to speak to you," I whispered.

He stood deliberately right in front of my face, so his cock was almost against it. "No problem, pass me the phone."

I couldn't.

"Hand me the mobile."

I knew Gary too well. He'd see this as an opportunity to say the wrong thing. And not by accident. He wanted to out me. Or at least hint at it.

"Princess," he said.

I feared what'd happen if my mother heard him repeat that and quickly placed the phone in his hand before I'd even thought it through.

"Hello, madam," he said, so full of politeness and charm.

But my mother wasn't Aunt Shauna.

"Yes, I do know him."

This was only going to end in disaster.

"Of course, yes."

I had visions of Betty and her husband trying to storm through the back door.

"Not at all. But the damage has been more serious than I feared."

I thought of the cucumber in my rear.

"Yes, it's taking a few hours to fix."

Just like my stretched sphincter, although I feared my reputation with my family and my neighbours may be irreparable.

"No, the money you left will be more than enough. I wouldn't dream of charging more."

I crossed my fingers, hoping my mother believed him.

"Why? Well, because I think of him as a friend."

What the hell was she saying to him?

"How long? Oh, several months. More. I've lost count."

What? Why was he telling her that? She didn't need to know I'd been keeping a friendship with an older man secret. I'd never be allowed to leave my home again! Or to go online unsupervised!

"Yes, I'll look out for him. I wouldn't let any harm come to him."

I hoped these were the reassurances she needed.

"He's like a little princess to me. Precious."

WHAT THE FUCK!?!

"She's away," Gary said, and held my mobile out to me. "Now she knows you're in good hands."

I was trembling as I took it off him. What the fuck had just happened? "Gary, why the hell did you tell her I'm like a little princess to you? I'm in shock."

"Because you are, because I get the sense your mother sees you the same delicate way and because it'll reassure her to know there's someone here who'll look out for you."

I was almost hyperventilating. "Did... Did she ask you if you were staying here?"

"No, no."

I looked up past his erection – God, he was actually loving this. "Gary, are you sure? Did you or she imply it?"

"No.

"She's smarter than she sounds, Gary. I know she sounds frantic, but-"

"You sound frantic, Princess, and there's no need to be." He crouched down, fixed a misplaced strand of hair away from my face, then kissed my cheek. "Now, baby, before we take a bath together, I want to have a conversation about your obedience." He took my hand. "Follow me."

CHAPTER 8

"Why have you brought me in here?" I asked, shaking.

Gary patted my behind. "So pert."

"Gary, why are we stood in my parents' bedroom?" I wanted to add that I found this exercise somewhat sick, but my nerves were so shattered from him speaking to my mother I was unable to find my tongue.

"Because your problem, Princess, is you're too quick to dismiss anything that's outside your comfort zone. And this room can be no greater test of going beyond your comfort zone."

I turned to him. "Gary, I don't want to do anything here. I don't even want to be here."

"Exactly," he said, then turned me again to face the bed. He leaned me forward until my palms were on the duvet. "I want you to stay like that until I tell you otherwise."

"Okay."

"Good girl," he said. "I don't need to tell you about the things I want to do to you, baby. You're much too intelligent a young girl to need me to explain." He parted my legs.

My naked clitty and she-balls hung out to dry.

He began to explore my rump. "Perhaps, it'd be easier if I explained to you that I've no wish to hurt you, or force you to do anything against your will."

"Ha," I said, much too quickly.

Gary froze his fingertips on my hole. "Excuse me?"

I still wanted to have a conversation with him about where things stood.

"Speak, Princess."

But not now. Not like this.

"You have my permission to speak candidly."

I breathed quietly in and out.

"Princess, I'm telling you to tell me what's bothering you."

"You know what," I snapped.

He sighed. "The conversation with your mother-"

"No! Well, yes. That too. But no, Gary, not that. I'm not happy you threatened to fuck my brains out." I could sense his ire at my language. "It was against my will. I didn't give you my consent."

He began to move his fingers again, gently rubbing the outside of my rectum. "I was pushing you, Princess."

"You were going to stick your cock in me, without a condom, and no doubt brutally fuck me, face down, on my bed."

"I wasn't. I was merely pushing your boundaries."

"I'm not convinced, Gary. I could sense it. I *knew* you were going to do it."

He removed his fingers. "I can promise you I wouldn't have done it, sweet cheeks... Not unless you'd told me to."

I most certainly would not.

"You could call it... Banter."

I wanted to look him right in the eye, but my legs were still shaky on my stilettos. "Gary, that was *not* banter. Not even close."

He moved alongside me. "I give you my word, I would not have had sex with you without your permission. And I'll never have sex with you without a condom. And I hope you'll never let any other man have sex with you without one."

Any other man? There were no other men!

"Princess, if you don't trust me now, you should tell me to leave."

I was staring dead ahead at the drawn blinds. I knew I couldn't tell him to leave. "You've nowhere to go."

"I can change my flight again," he said, as if he'd rehearsed the line. "I can take a taxi to the airport now."

I looked down. I shook my head. "I don't want you to go..." It was just that. "You..." Scared me sometimes.

"Excellent," he interrupted, standing behind me again.

"Then I've one simple question for you, baby."

I waited for it, already knowing I wasn't moving from this spot nor this position until he told me to.

"When are you going to start doing what I tell you?"

Bastard, I thought. What a fucking bastard.

"Because, Princess, let me explain exactly what you obeying me means to me..." He set his erection on my ass, sliding it into position over my rectum so my buttocks held it in place. "You can already *feel* what it does."

I swallowed saliva.

"I want to have absolute control over you, Princess. Not permanently. And not forever. But from a certain time of our agreement, beforehand, until a certain time afterward. Be it an hour or a day, it matters little. But I want it. I want you to willingly give this to me. And I want you to understand that I will expect- No, I will require you to obey me no matter what."

"I can't do that," I wheezed.

"Just listen, because I can guarantee I will not hurt you. Not properly hurt you. I may wish you to masturbate so furiously it feels almost painful, and I won't permit you to stop. But I will not do things to you that you ask of me not to beforehand. For example, if you tell me you're not ready for full sex, I will not and cannot order you to give yourself to me that way. Think of it as something of a safe word."

I was familiar with the term. Vaguely.

"If you tell me I cannot whip you with my belt, I will not order you to let me. I hope you understand. But if you are fully dressed and I order you to undress, you're to immediately do as I tell you. This is what I want. If I want you to go down on me, no matter how tired you are or how many times you've been down on me that day, I want you to diligently to it for me even if, no especially if, I can see the fatigue in your face. I want that devotion from you. It's not a need. I don't require this all day or even everyday. Perhaps not even every time I see you. But I want to experience it with you. This time. While I'm here. And preferably on a given day we can agree on."

I was listening.

"Will you devote yourself to my obedience on Wednesday, from the moment you wake until the moment you sleep?"

I was almost dizzy.

"You do not have to say yes now, Princess... But I do want you to."

"Gary, I'm not going to say yes... Yet... But I do have questions I need answered before I do."

"Ask away," he said.

I couldn't believe I was beginning to go along with this. It was more out of intrigue than anything, but part of me did feel aroused by the idea. Especially in these surroundings which should've been dissuading me. "They're more ground rules really, Gary. For the rest of today and tomorrow, I'd like to be able to add things I randomly think of."

"Add things?"

"To the list of things I won't be ordered to do."

"I'm agreeable to that, baby." He squeezed my cheeks.

I could feel him throb against me. "Like if Aunt Shauna shows up, the game is automatically suspended."

He said nothing.

"Gary, seriously. I won't have you ordering me to stay naked if she shows up or anything else which would destroy my reputation. If she shows up, the game is paused."

He pawed my hips.

"Gary, if you can't agree to this, we may as well call the game off now-"

"I agree, Princess... Spoilsport."

I started to turn my head, then I stopped. He'd told me not to move, after all.

"I was kidding. *You* set the rules in advance. But when the game begins, aside from Aunt Shauna showing up, nothing stops it... Okay?"

I took over a minute to think it all through in my head. This was perhaps a once in a lifetime opportunity. It was very possible I'd never see him again. I'd admitted aloud to him in the hotel that I was naturally submissive. It was definitely something I wanted to explore. And the day before on the path near the beach when he'd ordered me to walk in the open with my fly open it'd been both nerve-wracking and exhilarating.

"You don't have to decide now," he said.

I shushed him.

He waited.

There was also the fact he was impatient. He was used to getting his own way. What if my aunt Shauna did show up and he was too slow to alert me? Or he was in the middle of throwing a tantrum because the fantasy was shattered? This was a legitimate risk I had to consider. And one which was causing my clitty to unmistakeably grow. "I've made my decision, Gary."

He slid his cock out from between my buttocks and turned me to face him. "Let's hear it."

"There will be a lot of rules, serious ones which I don't want broken, but if you agree to them without pestering me... I will devote myself to obeying you for the entirety of Wednesday. I will literally behave as if I'm your property, and yours alone. No one else will ever have me this way."

Gary slipped his arms around me. "Oh, Princess, I can't begin to tell you how deliriously happy that makes me," he said, and pulled me down on top of him onto my parents bed.

Our erections grazed against each other.

Gary dragged my mouth to his, and slipped his tongue inside. He kissed me wildly, forcing goosebumps to erupt all over my body.

I felt the vigour transfer to my she-testes, as if I was ready to be milked for another orgasm already.

He stroked the soft skin of my back.

I kissed him back so passionately I could barely breathe, writhing my body against the superior might of his.

"I could so easily fall for you, Princess," he said finally.

"Fall for me?" I asked, feigning innocence.

"I could fall in love with you, baby. I mean that. I know it's a lot. But it's true. You're absolutely perfect. I've never in my life met anyone quite like you."

I blushed as my face lit up with legitimate joy. "Oh, Gary."

"I mean it... You're the one I want."

I stared into his eyes. "No, Gary... I'm the one you have."

CHAPTER 9

I squeezed my back against the taps in the warm bath, then gestured for Gary to join me.

He stood naked by the bath, his incredible body still glistening with a little leftover cum.

I moaned as I watched him. "I love your muscles," I whispered, drinking them in. "You're a real man's man."

His cock slapped against his thigh as he stepped one foot into the bath.

All I could think about was sex when I looked at him. There were so many moments I became crazed by my lust. I knew under the right circumstances I'd do anything with this man... Including give my virginity to him.

"For the rest of the week, I want us to take on traditional roles in this house," Gary said, taking position opposite me and allowing his groin to be swallowed up by the bubbles.

"What do you mean, lover?"

"Aside from us living as husband and wife..."

My clitty responded positively to the sound of that.

"I want you to take on the traditionally female chores around the house. You'll cook and clean. And I'll assume the male ones, Princess."

"Okay," I said, not giving it much thought. "I like the thought of waiting on you hand and foot."

He grinned.

"You're thinking naughty thoughts, Gary."

He nodded.

"Please share," I said, and gently pushed my foot between his legs until my toes made contact with his balls.

"I'm just picturing you bent over on your hands and feet, baby."

I groaned amorously. "I still can't believe you're here... With me."

"Me too."

I gave him a sarcastic look – he'd planned it, after all – but I let it go without comment. "I don't know how I'm going to survive letting you leave."

"Don't think about that now, Princess. This is only Monday. I don't go home till Saturday."

I didn't tell him, but his reference to somewhere else – with *someone* else – as home hurt.

"You're beautiful," he said.

I started to laugh.

"What, baby? You *are*. Don't you believe me?"

"Of course, Gary, yes. It's something else."

"What?"

I was still giggling, and had to cover my mouth. "I've just realised we left the cucumber in the bin... In the hotel room. Someone has to come along and empty that bin."

He leaned himself lower, allowing more water to run over his chest, matting his hairs. "It wasn't like we'd be using it again."

"Pity," I teased.

He grunted. "You do tempt me, Princess. Be careful. On Wednesday, you'll do whatever I tell you."

"Unless I make a ground rule against you shoving foreign objects inside me."

"You wouldn't."

"Actually, Gary, sorry. But I have to. I'm petrified at the thought of you using just any old thing as a dildo on me. That's an official rule. No foreign objects."

"Okay," he said.

"Sorry."

"It's fine, baby. The ground rules are there for a reason."

I blew him a kiss.

He blew one back.

I rubbed his balls with my foot. "I love how big they get." Like his body was constantly replenishing them with a fresh supply of sperm... For me.

Frustration funnelled across his face.

"They make me hungry." To swallow, I thought.

"I'd like to go out tomorrow," he said. "It's wonderful being here with you, baby, it really is, but spending so much time cooped up isn't good."

I tried to understand. He was on holiday, after all. "I can spare you for a couple of hours, Gary." Although I hated the thought of it.

"Are you joking, Princess? I've no intention of leaving you here on your own. You're coming with me."

I gulped. "Where?"

"Relax, you can go as Mark."

I cringed. "Please, *never* call me that. Ever." I hated how quickly my name made the mask of Princess slip away.

"Okay, honey."

"Where d'you want us to go?" I asked.

"We'll go shopping."

My innards stirred, hoping. "What for?"

"Do you have an Ann Summers store in the city?"

My insides leaped with joy. "Yes, Gary, we do!"

"We'll go there then, gorgeous."

"Oh, Gary, you're incredible. I can't wait to pick out some lingerie to wear for you. New stockings, suspenders, bras or even something more wild like a corset or basque! I can't wait, lover, honestly. You really know how to make a girl happy! You're so generous, spoiling me with your money!"

"Not exactly *my* money, Princess."

I hesitated. "Huh?"

"We'll be spending the money on the mantelpiece."

"The money my mother left for me? Oh, Gary, I'm not sure that's right-"

"Of course it is. Technically, it's my money."

"Yours?"

"I earned it, fixing your computer. Your mother told me to make sure I took it. *All* of it."

Had she really?

"And I'll spend it how I see fit."

I was a little ired, but I was also dying to go to Ann Summers with him. I smiled. "Okay, Gary... You're incorrigible."

"I know, Princess."

I started to wash my skin with a face cloth, deliberately cleaning off the last of our cum. "Goodbye, Gary sperm, I hope we meet again soon," I said, and moved my toes against his cock.

"You make washing me off you sound sinful, baby."

I bent my knees to reach my calves. "It feels it."

He stared at me for a couple of minutes as I went through the motions of washing myself. "I love the way you move, Princess."

I reluctantly stood.

"I'd just love to scoop you up on my thighs and fuck you so hard, Princess. Right here. Right now. You on top, facing me."

I feigned a gasp.

"I could make love to you in that position."

I giggled. "A little late to use the romantic language now, Gary."

"Sorry, honey, but I really hope you'll have sex with me before the week is over."

I ran the face cloth under my she-scrotum to my rear. "I'm still sore back there after the cucumber."

Gary shook his head. "I'm still somewhat shocked you let me use that on you."

"I did more than let you use it on me, Gary... I let you *fuck* me with it."

His cock pointed erect out of the water. "I could just order you to let me fuck you," he said.

"No, you couldn't," I said flatly. "We're not playing that game until Wednesday. You've two days to be patient."

His muscles tensed.

"Oh, I get it, big man. You could just take me now, against my will." I tossed the face cloth down into the middle of the bath, between his legs. "Good luck with that-"

Gary dove forward, taking my tiny she-penis into his mouth.

"Oh my God!" I shrieked.

He harshly grabbed my buttocks with his rough hands, holding me in place.

But I wasn't trying to get away.

His mouth felt wonderful on my sex.

I moaned and groaned.

He sucked me all the way in.

"That feels so good," I squealed. "So fucking good."

Gary grunted as he grazed my she-cock with his teeth. He showed me who was in charge, then switched back to the more sensual feel of his lips and his tongue sliding up and down on my clit.

I was delirious, and clung onto his powerful shoulders for support.

He drove his fingertips deeper into my flesh.

I cried out in ecstasy.

Gary frantically flung himself along my she-shaft, as if he was trying to face-fuck himself with her.

The water splashed between us.

I looked down at my lover.

He seemed to sense my gaze, and momentarily glanced up without conceding any of his pace.

"Don't you dare stop," I pleaded, as if somehow I too could read minds.

He struck my shaven base with his nose and my tiny she-balls with his chin.

Momentous pleasure reverberated within every part of my groin.

Gary snapped himself free.

I threw my palm towards my clitty.

"Oh no, you don't!" he said, and seized my wrist.

I threw my other hand down.

Gary grabbed it too.

"Let me get myself off, Gary, please!"

"No."

"But it's not even Wednesday yet."

He looked up, grinning, and shrugged. Then he watched for the next several minutes as my erection slowly but surely died away and my sex shrivelled down to nothing. He, meanwhile, remained stubbornly hard.

"You're evil."

"I'm hungry, Princess."

"Eat me," I pleaded, but I knew it was too late.

He laughed aloud, then let go of my wrists. "Don't touch her when I'm not looking. I mean it, baby. Keep yourself for later."

I reluctantly nodded. I'd obey him. For now. Even though it was outside of the day of our game. "I guess I'll go and get dressed before I make dinner."

"You do that, honey. But don't dress too much, if you know what I mean. I want you to be revealing in what you wear."

"Yes, Gary," I said, and stepped carefully out of the bath.

He swatted my buttocks. "Good girl."

CHAPTER 10

I picked out the ingredients I'd need for dinner and left them out on the kitchen counter. I wasn't a great cook. I wasn't a bad one either. But my repertoire was relatively limited, given I was 20 years old and mollycoddled by both my mother and father.

But what man could turn his nose up at a fat, juicy sirloin steak and skinny fries?

And if that didn't please him, I hoped the sight of me stood here naked but for a pair of stiletto heels would.

Where was he anyway?

Jeez, I couldn't be away from him for ten minutes.

"Gary?" I called, leaving the kitchen.

"In here," he said.

I stopped at the door to the bathroom and just watched him, smiling.

"What is it, Princess?"

"My man."

He was stood at the sink, shaving. He really looked the part of the man of the house.

"Don't laugh, lover, but I missed you."

He laughed, although his eyes remained fixed on the mirror.

I was only slightly disappointed to see he'd put his trousers back on. "Notice anything different about me?"

He spent the next few seconds finishing above his upper lip, then he glanced to me. His eyes rested on my crotch.

"Do you like it?" I asked, stroking a little red ribbon I'd found in the kitchen and tied around my clitty.

He nodded.

"You sure?"

He resumed shaving. "Very much so, Princess. It emphasises how you're my darling, little virgin... And sooner or later that ribbon's going to have to be undone..."

I smiled.

"Or cut."

I swivelled on my heels, as butterflies took to my stomach, and headed into my parents' bedroom.

"I was kidding, Princess!"

I knew he was, but sometimes a girl just enjoyed acting up. I opened my mother's wardrobe and took my time to peruse her collection. She had a lot of dresses. Unfortunately, the vast majority of them weren't to my personal tastes. Which was, to say the very least, slutty.

Gary left the bathroom and went into my bedroom.

I wanted to show off my smooth legs. I'd freshly shaven them before our bath. Surely there was something in here I could compromise on.

Minutes later, Gary exited my room and headed down the hall.

"Feel free to use the TV," I shouted after him.

He didn't answer.

I was starting to get annoyed. So many of these dresses resembled one word I hated to describe women's clothing – frocks. I was determined I'd never be seen in a frock. I wanted a sexy dress. Or even a skirt. Preferably short. I just couldn't find any-

There!

"Perfect," I said aloud, and lifted the hanger off the rack.

It was a beautiful, pink dress. It had buttons all the way down the front – perfect for when Gary decided it was time to devour me – and only knee length. Okay, it would stop just below my knees, but if I sat at the right angle I was sure I could hitch it higher. Especially when I crossed, uncrossed and recrossed my legs. Yes, I could make myself a right sexy, little vamp for him in this.

I decided my ribbon would be my only underwear, then

started to slip into the dress.

I became vaguely aware of voices, and assumed – without much thought – that he'd found the remote for the TV.

I took my time to do up the buttons, leaving the top two undone. I wasn't wearing a bra, so Gary would be able to reach inside and fondle my nipples any time he wished. I wondered if he'd even give me peace to cook before he started exploring me. I giggled as I hoped he wouldn't.

Hang on, those voices weren't coming from the TV.

There were two lower voices. Or perhaps voices further away. They were coming from outside. And there was a louder, nearer voice.

I recognised that voice!

"No, no, no," I said to myself quietly, and made for the window. I carefully peered between the blinds.

Out at the back of the house, Gary was stood talking over the wall. He was talking to the next-door neighbours! Betty and her husband Jim! The nosiest neighbours in the whole street!

I drew back from the window.

My pulse pounded.

My temperature rose.

And perspiration flowed.

Had he learnt nothing? Like, absolutely nothing?

I felt fury ripple through my body and my temples tightened as if I was about to have the most ferocious of migraines.

I stormed down the hall.

The kitchen door opened.

I came to a sudden halt in the hall.

The kitchen door shut.

I couldn't even call out to him in my feminine voice, in case he'd – and right now I'd put nothing past him – invited them in.

"Princess?" he said. "Where are you? I'm starving."

I barged into the kitchen like a hell whore on heels. "Are you out of your mind, Gary? I heard you. I *saw* you. What on earth were you thinking, going out there to chat to the neighbours?"

He looked at the steak. "Keep your panties on, honey..."

I already regretted not wearing any.

"All I did was empty the bin from in here. I took it outside. I told you I'd be doing the male chores this week."

I shook my head. "You don't do that. You don't go outside. I don't want anyone seeing you here."

"*I'm* the man of the house, Princess, get used to it."

"Yes, yes, yes, but you can't be seen here, Gary. Will you just listen to me for once?"

He looked at my dress with those sultry eyes.

"I appreciate you emptying the bin, but you should've left it for me to take out-"

"*I'm* the man of the house. The king of the castle. I'll be doing it *again*. This isn't up for discussion. *You're* the Princess. Know your place and fall in line."

I was breathless.

He brazenly walked over and gave me a gentle kiss on the lips, then he rubbed my sleeveless arms. "Relax."

I breathed.

"Everything's fine."

"It's just... Gary... You're not supposed to be here. That nosy cow next door tells my mother everything. She could be on the phone to Germany right now, repeating everything you've said to her."

He shrugged.

"Jesus, Gary, what on earth did you tell Betty and Jim?"

"Nothing," he said, then turned to walk into the living room. "Get a move on with dinner, woman, it's getting late."

I watched as he threw the door shut behind him.

CHAPTER 11

Gary was gone when I woke up on Tuesday morning. At first, I assumed he was merely in another room and I went to check, dressed only in my red ribbon. I dared peer through the blinds in the kitchen to make sure he wasn't outside again. There was no sign of him.

And then I realised he'd left me.

It wasn't much of a surprise. We'd barely spoken after dinner on Monday evening, as my anger over his actions that day threatened to boil over. And he was as pig-headed and stubborn as ever, silencing himself as he watched an old movie I couldn't understand and not even trying to initiate anything sexual at bedtime.

I checked through the blinds in the living room, but he wasn't out front either. And neither was my parents' car.

"Not again," I muttered.

I returned to my bedroom and checked my mobile.

MY MOTHER – Betty texted. She said Gary is a lovely gentleman. How do you know him? Hope he got your computer fixed. Let me know if you need more money. Your Aunt Shauna can drop some off for you xxx

ME – No, I haven't any plans to do anything. I should be okay. Enjoy the rest of your holiday x

I tried to tell myself Gary had only popped out for a newspaper. He was 47, 27 years older than me. People of that age had their daily habits.

And I'd mine. I wondered if I could sneak a quick wank into

my morning.

MY MOTHER – You didn't answer my question xxx

ME – He's a friend's dad x

Sure, what was one more lie now?

I decided to get dressed. My thong had been worn more than enough recently, so I tossed it into the wash – surely I'd be doing a wash before my parents got home, so I reasoned it'd be safe there for now.

I heard a car pull up outside and took a peak through my blinds.

It was Gary.

I pulled on a pair of jeans – no underwear was better than male underwear – then headed down the hall.

He walked through the front door.

"Hey," I said.

Gary shut the door, then turned around. He'd a newspaper under one arm and a bunch of flowers in the other.

I straightened my back and jutted out my bare chest.

"Princess," he started, sounding beleaguered, "I want to apologise for yesterday. I shouldn't have spoken to your neighbours when I knew it'd upset you. Then the way I ignored you for the rest of the evening, it wasn't right of me at all. I'd a rotten night's sleep because of my behaviour."

"I'd a bad sleep too, Gary."

He looked so handsome with the sun shining through the glass behind him. "May I ask for your forgiveness?"

"You're forgiven," I said, smiling.

"Thank you." He held out the flowers. "These are for you."

I took them from him. "I love them! No one's ever bought me flowers before... Obviously."

He leaned down to kiss my cheek. "Why don't you go get ready for our big day out?"

"Okay, lover." *Big* day out? What was going to be big about it? We were only going to quickly pop into the city to buy lingerie, after all.

CHAPTER 12

MY MOTHER – Which friend? xxx

I slipped my mobile back into my pocket, my plain fingernails catching my eye. "I'm tempted to make one of the rules for tomorrow that I can't answer my mother's incessant texts."

"I second that," Gary said, slowing the car so he could look for a parking spot.

"That'd be something, wouldn't it? Peace and quiet from her. Can I get that for my Christmas present instead?"

"Oh, Princess, if we're thinking about Christmas already, why don't you try to find a way to come see me? If you can afford the flights, I'll pay for the hotel."

How could I ever get away from my parents? "That's-"

"I'll even throw in a festive fuck."

I gasped.

"Or two, baby."

I gasped again.

Gary grinned. "You're too sweet."

"In all seriousness, lover, back to the rules... If my mother does text or call, you can't interfere with that. I need to be able to break from our fantasy to answer any way I see fit. You can't control that. It's too personal."

He sighed. "Okay... But I'm losing count of all these rules you keep thinking up."

I jokingly hit his arm. "It's not *that* many, Gary."

He reversed the car into a space. "At this rate, I'll barely be allowed to order you to do anything."

I cleared my throat. "I'm sure you've got plenty in store for me." My stomach was in knots at the thought of it. "But I agreed to this game, a whole day of it, and I want to make sure I please you... In every way I can."

He switched off the engine. "You will, Princess." He unfastened his seat belt. "Let's go explore the city."

The sun was blazing hot. The tarmac on the roads was melting. Lots of people were scantily-clad. And drivers seemed to be letting the heat go to their heads. I'd never heard so many horns hooting at once in all my life.

Gary didn't want to go straight to Ann Summers, and I was surprisingly comfortable being in public in his company as we window shopped for half an hour or so. Then we took a stroll through the grounds of city hall.

"Is there anywhere in particular you'd like to go, Gary?"

"The art gallery," he said. "I believe it's over there."

My heart sank as I followed his finger across the road. "Okay, *lover*," I whispered, despite the amount of people around us.

We crossed the road and entered the reception of an art gallery. The silence of the building was in stark contrast to the hustle and bustle outside.

"I researched this place online before I travelled," he said, as he led the way to an elevator. "The paintings I want to see are on the fourth floor."

I shrugged.

"I'd only make you take the stairs if you were wearing a short skirt."

I shushed him as I blushed.

The elevator doors closed behind us.

Gary pinned me against the wall, then shoved his tongue into my mouth.

I was powerless to resist him.

He slipped his hands up the back of my t-shirt and felt at the flesh of my back.

I was giddy as I kissed him back.

He pulled away a split-second before the doors opened again.

"Do not do that to me," I said breathlessly. "Unless you can guarantee you won't stop."

He swatted my tight ass as I walked out of the elevator. "You look so good in those jeans, Princess."

I was relieved to see the floor was almost empty, especially as something told me he wasn't going to keep his hands off me for very long.

"Wow," Gary said behind me.

I was flattered... Until I spun around and realised he was looking at a huge painting.

"That's an original Gauguin."

Who?

"Paul Gauguin, Princess, a French Post-Impressionist."

My only experience of impressionists was when Alistair McGowan was on the TV. His one of David Beckham was hilarious. He sounded just like him.

"It's breathtaking, don't you think? Absolutely magnificent. Such a genius use of colours."

All I saw was a hill with some trees.

Gary led me around several more paintings, as he rhymed off name after name which could've been the Italian football team for all I knew.

I knew nothing about art, and I was even beginning to get jealous that all his attention was on the work of these dead people and not on me. But, worse than that, I was getting bored. I'd thought today would be about me fighting my inner shyness and embarrassment as he held up garters, stockings, suspenders and the like for me to decide which ones I wanted to wear for him later.

"Paul Cézanne," he remarked.

I was staring at my feet, missing my stilettos.

"This must be worth twenty, thirty million pounds, Princess, maybe even more."

A woman in a hat looked at Gary, then at me. She walked on.

"Gary, will you please be careful when you call me that? That lady heard you."

He shrugged. "You're not embarrassed again, are you?"

I was actually more happy his eyes were finally back on me. "No, I'm just saying... Behave."

"Behave?" he asked. "How can I behave when I'm having the most amazing day out with the most beautiful girl in the world?"

I couldn't be angry with him. I smiled. Even though I didn't feel particularly girly. The only feminine item of clothing I was wearing was a bra. And I was paranoid that it could possibly be seen through my t-shirt. I decided I should make an effort, for his sake, and turned to face the Paul Cézanne painting-

Gary pinched the back of my bra through my t-shirt, then pulled back the elastic and let go.

It made a loud pinging sound I was certain everyone on the floor heard.

Gary stifled a snigger.

I made an angry face at him, even if I had to admit to myself I'd found that relatively amusing-

"Mark?"

CHAPTER 13

I turned around in horror.

"It *is* you! I knew it was you!"

Oh. My. God. "Elaine Bigelow," I said aloud, petrified she'd just witnessed Gary pinging my bra.

She hurried across the floor in her trainers, disturbing all remaining ambience in the room. "You're the last person I expected to see here." She looked at Gary. "Who's this?"

I blushed at her bluntness.

"I'm Gary," he said forcefully, and thrust out a hand. "A friend."

Elaine shook it. "Pleased to meet you. I went to school with Mark. We're old friends."

We were *not* friends.

"I see," Gary continued. "Well, any friend of this delightful human is a friend of mine."

Delightful human? I was aware I'd told him never to call me Mark, but that was a ridiculous alternative.

"What brings you to this place, Mark?" Elaine asked.

"I did," Gary said, and glanced again at the Paul Cézanne. "I've more than a passing interest in art. Yourself, Elaine?"

"I'm between years of an art course, but to be honest I've been here ten minutes and I'm bored already."

I was certain she just tried to examine my chest with her eyes.

"What about you, Mark?"

"I'm unemployed... At the moment."

"Well, that's okay."

"I know, Elaine."

Gary gave me a subtle look of disapproval.

I recognised it from the way my parents looked at me when someone asked what I worked at.

"Have you guys been here long?"

"About an hour," I said.

"We were just about to leave," Gary added.

We were? "Yes, Elaine, we were. But it was good to see you-"

"Say, I've no plans and it's a really warm day today, would you two care to join me for an ice cream?"

Absolutely not. But my tongue twisted.

Gary was silent.

"Come on," Elaine said. "You can tell me how you two met."

Did she *know*? She couldn't. Surely, she couldn't.

"Okay," Gary said. "We're about done here anyway."

I made eyes at my lover that said *I'm sorry*.

"It's okay," he mouthed back.

The elevator doors opened.

Elaine walked out to the reception first.

Gary pinched my bum.

The three of us headed out of the art gallery to the street.

"I can't wait to get a good catch-up with you, Mark."

"You too, Elaine," I lied.

Gary spotted a street vendor selling ice-cream and led us across the road.

Elaine ran ahead.

"Gary, I'm so sorry. I'd no intention of this happening."

"Don't be silly, Princess. She seems nice enough."

I was hesitant to tell him Elaine and I hadn't ever really been the best of friends.

Gary and I walked together, our hands almost touching, until we caught up with Elaine, who'd already got herself an ice-cream.

Gary bought two for us, and placed mine in my hand.

"Thank you, Gary," I said.

"You're welcome."

I licked mine, then turned to Elaine. "So, I don't think we've seen each other since we left school, what's been happening?"

"Oh, all sorts, Mark, you know me..."

I did.

"Usual drama. Cheating boyfriends. Arguing parents. I've gone from one dead-end part-time job to another..."

I was surprised, she actually wasn't bragging. Perhaps she had matured.

"And my brother came out of the closet last year."

An awkward silence hung in the air.

She quickly looked between us. "Not that there's anything wrong with that kind of thing!"

"Of course not," Gary said.

The traffic lights next to us turned green.

"Mum and dad weren't too pleased, at first. Especially dad. But mum's come around. And dad's, well, dad. But he's learning to live with it. And, you know me, my brother will always be my hero no matter what."

I nodded, deciding not to tell her I'd nearly forgotten she even had a brother.

Gary wiped cream from the side of my mouth. "You missed a bit."

I felt my face redden. "Thanks."

Elaine looked at us both again.

I knew what she thinking.

"So, tell me, how do you two know each other?" She licked her ice-cream. "What's the deal here?"

"Deal?" I asked. "There's no deal, Elaine. Gary's a friend."

"Yes," he added.

"Oh, wait, I didn't mean to- Sorry, I'm a nosy cow. I apologise. I'll shut up now and mind my own business. I'm sorry, Gary, Mark can tell you what I was like in school. Always railroading myself into other people's business and saying the wrong thing."

"It's okay, Elaine, no harm done."

She seemed nervous as she looked around herself.

I wanted to finish my ice-cream as quickly as possible, then go shopping for some sexy lingerie. My tiny clitty tingled within my red ribbon at the thought.

"I still live at home," Elaine said finally. "Do you still live at home, Mark?"

"Yeah."

"It's a lovely home," Gary said.

Why the hell did he say that?

"It is," Elaine agreed.

"Elaine, listen we have to-"

"No, don't worry. I understand." She held her ice-cream out from herself, then went to hug me with her other arm.

I did the same.

"Gary," she said, and hugged him.

"Elaine, nice to meet you."

"I'll maybe see you around, Mark."

I half-waved her off. "Take care, Elaine."

She trotted off on her trainers, looking a little lost.

I patted Gary's arm and nodded in the opposite direction.

We started to walk.

As I'd planned, we were going in the direction of Ann Summers.

"Princess," Gary said, "she knows."

I said nothing.

CHAPTER 14

We sat on a bench in the middle of a cobbled, pedestrian-only street, our backs to the Ann Summers lingerie store.

My excitement had given way to my nerves.

"You *can* do this," he said, his hand resting next to mine.

"I can't, I'm sorry."

He rubbed my little finger with his. "Why not?"

"Because I'm terrified, Gary."

Throngs of people filtered by in either direction.

"I'll be with you. I won't leave your side. I'll act properly, I promise. I won't make any jokes or do anything to embarrass you."

"Thank you, but I still don't think I can do it." I dared turn to look him in the eye. "You go in, on your own. I trust your judgement."

He sighed. "I really think you should come with me. It'll build your confidence. In there, lies everything you are... Who you want to be. Don't give up now."

I turned even further, and looked over his shoulder into the shop window. There was some incredibly sexy outfits on the mannequins. Extremely revealing items. Classy items. Slutty items.

"Picture yourself wearing those things," he said.

My clitty tingled. "I am. I really want to."

"I'll worship you, Princess."

I almost shushed him. There were too many people around to be talking to me like that. "What if someone who knows me sees us? Again?"

"There's more chance of someone you know seeing you out

here in the street. Wouldn't you rather be in there, picking out the things you know you'll love?"

I reluctantly nodded.

He leaned his mouth to my ear. "Then we can go home and you can wear them for me tomorrow... When I order you to."

I giggled. "I don't want to wait that long. I want to wear them for you tonight."

"So, is that a yes then?"

I took a deep breath. "Yes, Gary, but let's go quickly before I change my mind."

The other customers kept their heads down when we walked in, but the staff all looked over.

I felt extremely intimidated.

Gary cleared his throat.

I sensed he too was nervous, and that did nothing to allay my fears.

We just stood at the entrance like two ducks out of water.

Gary pointed to our left, then started to walk behind a walled display of clothing in different sizes.

I quickly followed, relieved in the slightest that it took us out of view of the staff. However, we were also right at the window. I kept my back to it.

"That's sexy," he whispered, running his fingers over the lace material of a bra and thong set on a mannequin.

My first instinct was to tell him to buy it, I'd meet him outside and we'd go home.

"Can I help you?" asked a female member of staff.

"No, thank you," Gary said.

I turned crimson.

She nodded, then turned around and walked off.

"It's like they know, Gary," I whispered.

"Then they know how lucky I am."

I couldn't even muster a smile. "That isn't helping."

"Sorry, Pr-" He stopped himself.

I was stood so close to him that it probably made us look like a couple, but I also felt more comfortable with him than away from him.

"Look, for all they know we're buying a gift for someone else."

I tried to believe that, as my eyes took suddenly to something I instantly fell in love with. "Gary..." I moved in front of him and felt the fine fabric of a white lace basque. It had matching white thong panties and white stockings too. The basque had built-in suspenders. "I... I'd like to get this."

He looked at the outfit and nodded. Then he lowered his lips to my ear. "Are you sure you're not just saying that so we get the first thing we see and leave?"

"No, honestly."

He smiled. "I do like it, though. Very much so."

A couple spoke in hushed voices on the other side of the wall behind the display.

I found my size on the rack, and thrust the items into his hands. Mine were shaking too much to hold onto anything.

He studied the colour.

I knew the implication too.

"Yes," he said. "Definitely this."

Even the label said it... Virgin white.

The price tag also suggested my mother's money from the mantelpiece – in Gary's wallet – wouldn't leave much change for anything else. Which meant we could immediately go home.

Gary started to walk further on, deeper into the shop, in the direction of the till.

My mobile beeped in my pocket. I knew who it'd be.

MY MOTHER – I asked you a question. Which friend is Gary's son? Do I know him? Xxx

ME – Chris. You don't know Chris xx

I didn't even have a friend called Chris. I put my mobile away, then looked up. Where was Gary?

He cleared his throat, then nodded for me to follow him.

The staff watched me walk across the floor, past the till and towards Gary.

He'd found something else.

I stood in front of the item, deliberately blocking the staff's view. Although I was pretty sure they knew their shop layout well enough to know exactly what he was showing me... A pair of red crotchless panties.

"Yes?" he asked subtly.

I nodded.

He turned the tag over to check the price.

"We don't have enough," I said.

"I do. Consider it my treat..."

Another customer breezed by my back.

"I want to spoil you."

I felt perspiration under my bra strap.

Gary walked on.

I sheepishly lagged behind, then I felt scared and caught up. "Don't leave me on my own," I said quietly.

His eyes spotted something.

I cringed as he lifted a pair of nipple clamps.

A man nearby was uncomfortably giggling as a woman in his company showed him a vibration setting on something I couldn't see.

"Perhaps for tomorrow," Gary said, and set the nipple clamps in his same hand as the lingerie.

"I think we've enough now, Gary."

He turned around, and headed back in the direction of the till.

I hesitated, then followed.

To my dismay, he walked past the till.

I drew alongside him. "Where are you going?"

"Up there," he said, and gestured to stairs which led to a second floor.

I gulped. Oh God.

"Can you not put that on silent?"

I hadn't even heard my mobile beep again.

MY MOTHER – Chris who? Xxx

"You first," Gary said.

I reluctantly started on the stairs, knowing Gary would be looking up at my ass as we climbed.

ME – I don't know. I don't know him very well. The computer's fixed. Forget about it xx

I was shocked when I slipped my phone back into my pocket and looked up. The second floor was more like an out-and-out sex shop than a lingerie store. I could barely believe how sordid some of the items were.

"This is more like it," Gary said. "Maybe you'll relax a little."

What?

"No customers up here."

He was right!

"No staff either."

I reached my palm into his free hand and squeezed. "I'm sorry, you've no idea how much this is taking out of me."

He squeezed mine back. "I'm proud of you, Princess."

I found courage within and kissed his lips.

He started to slide his tongue.

I pulled away, but only because of the way I was dressed. "Later," I promised. "And then much, much more." I patted his crotch. "I'm going to swallow."

Gary looked surprised as he broke into a huge smile.

I started to look amongst the items. There was more than this girl could take in. Sex toys. Dozens of sex toys.

"We're not leaving without one," he said.

As long as I could slip outside while he took one to the till, I was okay with that. I was more than okay with that. In fact, I already had my eye on a ridiculously huge, black vibrator.

Gary investigated another mannequin.

I dared wrap my fingers around the shaft. I couldn't help but compare it to the cucumber.

"No," Gary said firmly.

"What?"

"You're not getting that one, pick another."

"Why?" I asked, although his forceful tone was a turn-on that made me look forward to tomorrow.

"It's too big. I'm not using anything on you that'll leave you too sore for me."

I gasped. Or, rather, I feigned a gasp. It was as if the moment we'd agreed on the virgin white lingerie we'd entered into a private, unspoken agreement that I'd lose my virginity to him before the week was over.

I kept looking at the various vibrators, aroused to know he wanted me to pick one. One he'd use on me. I certainly wasn't making a rule banning that for tomorrow.

Gary, meanwhile, was looking at a leather collar and chain leash on the mannequin.

I said nothing when he found the same set on a table next to the mannequin and put them in his hand.

He moved on to another display.

My eyes drifted again to the monstrous vibrator he'd chastised me for almost choosing. I couldn't help but wonder what it'd feel like to try to deep-throat it. Perhaps I could find something similar, maybe just one size down.

"This too," Gary said, and held up a butt plug. "You can wear it next time we go walking."

"Wear it?" I asked innocently.

"Inside you."

My pulse thudded faster.

"See how shapely it makes you when I give you a little public spanking."

I caught my gasp in a sudden intake of air.

Gary glanced down the stairs. "Pick a dildo, Princess, before anyone joins us."

Gary trudged off the bottom step of the stairs.

I quickly followed behind, clutching the vibrator by the

shaft, as people – staff and customers alike – looked at me. I felt like such a sissy whore.

He walked towards the till.

"Gary," I said, raising my voice.

He looked at me, his hands full of every other item he intended to purchase.

"Can you take this?" I wanted desperately to run outside and spare myself the embarrassment of having to go to the till with a dildo in my hand.

"No," he said, and clearly he couldn't.

Shame shook my body from head to toe as I walked across the shop floor, shaft in hand. A gentle breeze blew from the open front door. I glimpsed passers-by looking in, then averted my eyes.

Gary placed the lingerie, accessories and devices on the counter.

I couldn't set my dildo down quick enough. It was so life-like. Bulging veins and bulbous head.

"Is that everything?" asked the girl at the till.

I swore she was smirking, as if sarcastically implying we hadn't enough.

"Yes," Gary said, and removed his wallet.

I stared at the floor, certain my red face was giving everyone the answer to the question on their minds – *is that older guy fucking the younger one?*

I defiantly looked up as the girl rang our purchases through the register.

The number on the till kept going up and up. It was becoming an absurd total. What if Gary and I didn't actually see each other again? It seemed like such a waste if we didn't.

I saw myself deep-throating my new dildo after he returned home on Saturday. I'd have to find a good hiding place in my bedroom for all these things. Somewhere my snooping mother would never think of looking. I guessed I'd worry about that later.

Gary paid.

The girl passed two big branded bags along the counter.

"You get them," Gary said to me.

I reluctantly lifted them.

"Let's go."

I followed him out of the shop and into the daylight.

Gary crossed the cobbled street and led us straight into a bar.

"What're you doing?" I asked, as the smell of cigarette smoke hit my nostrils. "I thought we were going straight home." To play.

Loud music thudded out from speakers.

"We are," he said, then pointed to the bathroom. "But first I want you to go in there and insert the butt plug."

"What?"

He leaned down to my ear. "C'mon, Princess, imagine how hot it'll be when you've to walk back to the car with that thing inside you."

CHAPTER 15

I locked the cubicle door behind myself, then set down the shopping bags and sifted through them until I found the butt plug. I lowered my jeans to my ankles as I studied it. 4 insertable inches of silicone. I shivered as I thought about trying to walk the distance back to the car with it inside me.

There was only one thing for it. I brought it to my mouth and began to lick around the circumference. It wouldn't be enough. I needed more lube. Natural lube. I shoved the whole thing inside my mouth and tried to drench it in my saliva.

I pressed one hand on the cubicle wall for support as I bent over, readying myself for the penetration. My little clitty hung lifeless in her red ribbon.

I ensured I'd coated the plug in all the saliva I could muster, then I carefully swapped it from the opening of one orifice to the opening of another.

I took a deep breath, then started to apply pressure on my anus. I was pleasantly surprised when my hole opened so easily. It was as if it had an eagerness about it.

I exhaled in an emotional, sissy-like manner, as my sex twitched into life below. My heart began to beat faster. I liked this. I really did. I was meant to take things inside myself.

I started to slide the plug in and out, as my saliva quickly dried into the recesses of my rectum.

The main door to the gentlemen's toilets swung open.

I froze, mid-stroke.

Footsteps crossed the floor.

My she-shaft was erect, stretching the ribbon.

A man unzipped his fly, then urinated.

My sphincter puckered around the plug.

He seemed to take forever, as if he'd downed several pints before this toilet break.

My anus slowly started to expel the sex toy, against my will. I steeled my teeth together, searching for silence, and forced it all the way back in. My fingernails slid momentarily down the cubicle wall.

The man finally finished, zipped up his fly and walked out of the bathroom without washing his hands.

I crouched down to collect my jeans, pulled them carefully up and positioned them in place, zipped myself up and fastened my belt buckle.

I clenched my buttocks before I unlocked the door and took my first tentative steps with a butt plug jammed up my asshole.

Oh, how I imagined doing this again but in a pair of huge stiletto heels, ensuring my walk was even sexier.

The sensations as I walked were insanely intense, sending waves of opposing discomfort and pleasure through my innards.

I staggered against the hand basins, and clutched them for balance. How the hell was I supposed to walk all the way out to the bar, never mind back to the car?

It wasn't Wednesday yet. Gary didn't have the right to order me to do anything. There was nothing to stop me from going back into the cubicle and removing the toy.

Nothing... Except the incredible hold he had over me.

I opened the door which led back to the bar.

CHAPTER 16

Every step I took created new shocks throughout my form. There was no way I could make it all the way back to the car with this inside me.

I saw Gary sat at a table with a pint of Guinness in front of him and a glass of white wine, presumably for me. I was actually relieved we weren't immediately leaving.

He smiled as I approached.

"It's in," I said.

"Good," he said, and watched as I apprehensively looked at the wooden chair.

Couldn't he have found us a couple of soft seats?

Gary had a cruel glint in his eye.

No, of course he'd chosen these seats. Deliberately so. I tried to compose myself before I attempted to ease my ass onto the wood.

"People are looking," he said. "If only they knew."

My ass was jutted out. My palms were on the table. And I was making the manoeuvre in slow-motion.

"That's it, nice and easy."

I squirmed as my jeans made contact with the chair.

Gary groaned. "Amazing."

It was almost agonising to ease more of my weight onto my rear. My knuckles were turning white, as I gripped the edge of the table. I couldn't hide the grimace from my face.

"You turn me on so much," he whispered.

I started to shush him, then gasped as pain pierced my rectum. I suppressed my exhalations into a series of grunts, as I let the last of my weight transfer from my hands and feet to my rear.

Gary pushed my wine forward. "Try this."

I took an eager swig, yet I felt no relief.

"This is a nice bar."

My attention was focused only on the trauma in my tail end.

"I like being at home with you, but it's good to get out."

My mind was all over the place, as I thought I saw Gary take his mobile out from his pocket. "Yes, it is." But I'd be relieved to get home where I could live out my pain more freely.

Gary tapped a button.

I felt a tingling sensation within my anus.

Gary watched me.

"Oh my God, Gary, something's wrong. Something's happening."

He had that all-too familiar devilish look on his face.

I looked to his hand again as vibrations rocketed within my rectum. That wasn't his mobile. "Gary, what is *that*?"

"I didn't think you noticed it in the shop."

I gulped.

"I swiped it up from the counter before the girl could put it in one of the bags."

My innards ricocheted off the plug. "What... What is it?"

"It's the remote control, silly. It has different settings for vibrations." His thumb hovered over the plus button. "Watch." He tapped it.

My eyes crossed, my legs flailed and I'd to physically cover my mouth to stop from squealing.

"I'm not sure how high it goes, five I think," he said. "Should I keep going?"

I threw my head from side-to-side, then stopped suddenly as my hole succumbed to sheer brutality she wasn't made to take. I dug my elbows into the table and leaned forward to ease the pressure inside.

"Are you leaning forward for a kiss, Princess? Here? In public?"

I couldn't speak.

"Okay, baby." He leaned forward.

I'd to drop myself off my elbows and onto my ass to avoid his lips. I physically cried out.

Several people turned around.

I buried my mouth around the rim of my wine glass.

Gary's thumb was no more than an inch above the plus button.

"Please don't," I whispered. "I can't take anymore."

"I disagree-"

I threw my fingers to his wrist. "No, please. I can't. Not..."

"Yet?" he asked.

I reluctantly nodded. It was the only way to placate him. Even though I'd intended to tell him *not here*. I squirmed on my chair, aiming my ass off the edge, and crossed my legs to control the pre-cum beginning to leak from my clitty.

"I'm warning you, Princess, do not let it slip out."

"I wish I could... It's firmly wedged up there now."

"Good," he said, and switched it to the next higher setting.

"Fuck!"

Several more people looked over.

A passing barman stopped at our table. "Are you okay?" he asked.

I tried to nod, but my reaction was more like a tremble.

"She's fine," Gary said.

The barman looked confused. He hesitated, then toddled off with several empty pint glasses in hand.

My eyes were watering.

"That's level three. I think the label said it goes up as high as five... We'll just have to see."

As the song playing throughout the bar drew to a close, the volume fell lower than the voices of the other customers.

"I can *hear* it," Gary said. "I can actually hear it vibrate."

I threw my eyes to the bathroom. I needed to get there and remove this thing before Gary eroded all sense of self-respect I had left.

"You'll never make it, Princess..."

The next song began with a thunder of drums.

"And, even if you look like you're going to, I'll just double-tap this all the way up to level five... And you'll find yourself lying on the floor, a crumpled mess."

I squeezed his wrist. "Please don't do that, Gary. Don't torture me. I'll stay here. I'll try to find a way to take it at level three. Just, whatever you do, don't press that button again."

He sighed, then shook his head. "Are you *really* trying to tell me what to do?"

"No, no, no... I'm pleading... I'm begging!" I realised I was becoming so animated it was obvious to anyone watching that this man held some serious control over me.

And people *were* watching.

His thumb moved over the button again.

I shook my head in disbelief.

Gary set down the remote instead. "Don't dare touch that, Princess." He downed a huge swallow of his pint. "Or you'll be walking to the car at level five."

The vibrations reverberated up my spine and down all four legs of the chair. I couldn't take anymore and tossed my long, blonde hair forward, veiling my face from the people watching.

"Look at me."

I couldn't function.

"Now, Princess."

I couldn't move.

He removed his hand from the pint.

I watched in shock as he took hold of the remote again.

"Another lesson for tomorrow," he said, and upped the setting to level four.

I forced a catastrophic wail into a whimper.

"Don't defy me, Princess."

My entire body was a prisoner to both the invader within and the devil across the table.

"Look at me," he said.

I forced my thudding head ever so slightly higher until I could see him through the cascading, vibrating locks of my hair.

"Good girl."

I glanced to the remote. "Turn... It... Down... *Please*."

He shook his head, then supped more of his pint.

"You... Can... Turn... It... Back... Up... Again... Later."

Gary looked around the bar as if I wasn't even there. Except for the pride on his face. The pride he felt at the anguish and humiliation he was causing me. He revelled in it. It was his absolute thing.

And only the pre-cream oozing from my sex arched me all the way from anger to adoration for this incredible, yet heinous, cruel man.

"I know you're close," he said.

I was close to losing my mind.

"Close to climaxing. I can see it." He laughed. "Hell, I can feel it, vibrating across the floor from your chair to mine. If I can feel it, Princess, you can guarantee there are others here who feel it too... Have you no shame?"

I tried to speak, but could only make hoarse utterings.

"I wonder were any of them customers in Ann Summers when we were there."

I stared through my hair at him.

"They must've had questions about the relationship between you and I."

I watched him position his thumb over the button. I shivered as I shook my head. Pylons of pain stacked atop each other within the vibrating walls of my rectum. I didn't feel I'd survive the final level. I had to try to stop him.

Gary's thumb fell towards the button.

I tried to reach out.

He pressed.

My hand hit my glass, spilling my wine over the table as orgasmic greatness superseded the blinding excruciation in my asshole.

Gary watched.

I emptied my she-balls of load after load of lady juice into my jeans.

His thumb stayed clear from the minus button, ensuring the unwavering continuation of my torture.

Even as my orgasm subsided.

Pleasure was suddenly plundered once more by an avalanche of agony in my rear.

I couldn't take it. I'd lost all self-control. My body was nothing more than a quivering wreck. And I fell sideways to the floor from my chair.

As countless customers watched.

My body convulsed.

Gary double-tapped the minus button, negating my trauma down only to the level three setting. He left the remote on the table, then took himself to one knee, helping me up from the floor.

I was putty in his hands.

"I think you've had enough," he said.

I'd had more than enough, and craved further respite from the vibrating onslaught within.

"Definitely," agreed the barman, taking hold of me by my other arm. "Time you two were leaving."

They stood me up on my two feet.

Yet my ass continued to jut out, shaking like jelly from within.

Gary mercifully hit the minus button once more, then stuffed the remote in his pocket. "Thank you," he said to the barman. "We'll be leaving now."

CHAPTER 17

Despite somehow convincing Gary to switch off the vibration setting on my butt plug, I was still staggering from street to street beside him.

"Stop it," I snapped.

"What?" he asked, his tone the most insincere of innocence.

"You're enjoying this, seeing me struggle."

"I could sweep you up in my arms and carry you back to the car."

I stopped so I could lean against a wall. "I need a breather."

"How bad is it?"

I huffed and puffed. "It's not that it's bad, Gary, it was just *so* intense back in that bar. I still can't believe you did that to me. Everyone was looking at me."

"They thought you were drunk."

"Ha! Don't kid me, Gary. I'm sure they thought I was having some sort of epileptic orgasm. *I* thought I was having some sort of epileptic orgasm!"

A guy in a baseball cap looked at me as he walked past.

I handed Gary one of the Ann Summers bags. "Please, take this."

He dutifully took it from me. "Would you like me to carry both of them?"

"No."

A slowing double-decker tour bus obscured half the sunlight from our side of the street.

I tried to channel my breathing.

"You really came, didn't you?"

I nodded.

"Astounding, Princess."

I looked at him, trying to shoot a look of disapproval, but I couldn't help concede a grin. "I couldn't control myself. I was a complete slave to this thing inside me."

"*My* slave," he said.

"Tomorrow, lover... Not until then."

Gary slid the remote out of his pocket. "Excuse me?"

I closed my eyes and concentrated hard on relaxing the walls of my anus around the plug.

"That's what I thought, Princess."

I opened my eyes in time to see him slip it back into his pocket.

"Let's go."

I reluctantly followed behind him, echoes of my onslaught in the bar ricocheting in my hole with every additional step.

"Gary," I said, stopping outside the window of a fashion store.

He turned around. "You need *another* break?" He gestured ahead. "It can't be more than a few minutes to the car."

"It's not that." I pointed into the window. "It's *that*."

"The whole outfit?"

"No, Gary, just the skirt. It looks amazing. It's short. It's leather. Look at the split at the side. I know you've already spent so much on me today, but... Would you mind buying me that skirt?"

He looked hesitant as he scratched his head.

"I'll make it worth your while," I whispered, leaning my body up against his. "*Really* worth your while."

"How so, Princess?"

"If you buy it for me today, I might just wear it somewhere outdoors for you."

He looked lustfully down at me. "Really?"

I bit my lower lip, then nodded.

"I need you to promise."

I gazed at the skirt again. It was wonderful. I knew how sexy I'd feel in it. How confident. How racy. How daring. "I promise...

So long as it's somewhere secluded, not public. I only want to be seen by you."

He nodded, then passed me the other Ann Summers bag. "I'll be back in a minute."

Gary walked out of the fashion store with a shopping bag in hand.

Yet I knew that face. "How much?" I asked, fearful of his response.

"More than I make in a day."

I placed my palm on his wrist and squeezed. "Thank you."

He opened the bag to let me look inside.

I smiled. "Oh, Gary, I love it. It's wonderful. I really will make it worth your while. Thank you so much."

"Okay, I guess we should head back to the car."

We started to walk together, side-by-side, much closer than we had been and with my junk still stuffed full of the butt plug. I felt I deserved the treat, especially after what he'd put me through in the bar. Even if I did know I'd be reliving that experience for years to come. I just hoped I could keep my promise about wearing such a provocative, sexy skirt outdoors for him.

"Mark! Gary!"

We stopped in our tracks.

"Yoohoo!"

We turned around.

"What a delight to see you again," Aunt Shauna said, rushing up towards and gazing at Gary.

"My pleasure entirely," Gary said back, yet I could see the frustration on his face.

"You like to keep this one close at hand, Mark."

Whatever did she mean?

"You two been shopping?" Aunt Shauna's eyes went from the bag in Gary's hand to the two Ann Summers' ones in mine.

My face flooded red.

"Oh my," she said, then looked back and forth between us

both as if the penny had finally dropped.

"I..." I imagined the subsequent, hysterical phone calls between Aunt Shauna and my mother. "Can..." Then the rage I'd face from both my parents after. "Explain..." The ejection from my home. "Aunt..." The excruciation of being disowned. "Shauna."

She was waiting.

Gary was offering no way out for me.

"I got some... *Things*... For my new girlfriend."

Aunt Shauna raised one eyebrow and looked down on me, as if to say *don't lie to me, you sissy, little shit.*

Gary burst out laughing. "Oh, stop being such a princess and tell your aunt the truth."

The truth!?!

Aunt Shauna gazed at me with a shocked look on her face.

I was stunned into silence.

Gary slipped his hand into his pocket.

"What's the truth?" Aunt Shauna demanded.

Gary tapped the plus button.

"Mark, what's going on?"

My anus went into immediate convulsions.

Gary tutted.

I was beyond jittery as my buttocks attempted to gyrate, despite my efforts to clench them shut and hold my thighs still.

"Shauna," Gary began calmly, "we didn't tell Mark's mother exactly how he downloaded the virus."

For once, the sound of my birth name from his lips was the least of my problems.

"Uh-huh, go on."

"But I'm sorry to say he watches pornography."

I felt like I was going to pass out.

"Loves it, in fact. Can't get enough. Loves all kinds of stuff."

Big cocks. Semen-soaked faces. Cum dribbling out from well-fucked assholes.

Aunt Shauna looked both shocked and disgusted.

My mouth remained shut. My teeth locked together. And the

butt plug buzzing within my rectum.

"But being a fussy, little princess as usual, was too scared to go in and buy a tape alone, so dragged me along for company."

Aunt Shauna was puffing for breath.

"Ended up buying several," Gary added.

My nostrils flared and my eyes widened as Gary tapped the plus button a second time.

"At least this way there's no chance of the computer getting another virus, Shauna."

Aunt Shauna appeared to be having palpitations.

My own heart was keeping the same symptoms in the family, as my back and bum drenched in perspiration.

"Show your aunt the films you bought."

I couldn't believe it.

"Open the bags and show her."

I looked at my lover, dumbstruck.

His hand moved again in his pocket.

I knew I couldn't contain the third setting. I slackened my grip on the bags. Even if it meant letting her glimpse inside... Anything but another attack on my anus.

"That won't be necessary!" Aunt Shauna declared loudly, then pushed her way between us and stormed off.

I couldn't even bring myself to turn and watch her go.

"Say thank you, then, Princess."

"What!?!"

He hit the minus button twice in his pocket.

The butt plug ceased vibrating. I *was* thankful for that, at least. However... "Gary, what the hell were you thinking, telling my aunt I love porn, all different sorts? And you came with me so I could get a whole collection of tapes?"

He stifled a laugh.

"It's not funny! This is my life!"

"Don't get your ribbon in a twist, Princess, it was warranted."

I was furious. How dare he try to justify destroying my life!

"Baby, I had to say something or she was going to look in one of those bags. She didn't believe for a second you had a girlfriend."

I stared him out.

"No offence."

Some – okay, a little – taken.

"You're *my girl*," he said quietly, with a glint in his eye.

I tried not to let it work with me. Not now. Not yet.

"There was no way she was going to look in the bags when she thought they were full of pornos."

"You should've thought of something else, Gary!"

"Like what?"

"Anything!"

"Such as?"

I exhaled loudly.

"Exactly. She was seconds away from ripping those bags from your hands and your cushy, little life as you know it would've been over. You should be thanking me."

I raised my eyebrows. "You switched the plug on again!"

He giggled, then held up his hands. "Okay, you got me. I apologise. That was me getting carried away... Again."

I sighed. "Let's go."

Gary started to follow me.

I shoved my hand into his pocket and hauled out the remote. "I think it's best I keep hold of this, for the time being."

He shrugged.

We walked on, blending in as best we could with the rest of the city's shoppers. Gary's walk normal. Mine compromised by the menace inside me.

"Look on the bright side," Gary began, "your aunt Shauna won't be bothering us again."

I wasn't so sure. I checked my mobile. Nothing.

Yet.

CHAPTER 18

I was in the outhouse at the back of the garage, putting clothes belonging to both of us in the washing machine. After I'd gone commando for our shopping trip and blown my load in spectacular fashion in the bar, my jeans definitely needed a clean. I found my thong in the wash basket and made a mental note not to forget to separate it from my male clothes when the wash was finished. The last thing I needed was for my mother to find girly underwear when she came home.

After all, as Aunt Shauna had proved, no one would believe I was capable of having a girlfriend – least of all, me.

I hurried back to the house, diving in through the back door before Betty or Jim next door spotted me and instigated an impromptu chat.

Gary was stood in the kitchen, the shopping bags at his feet. "You should find somewhere to keep all this, Princess."

"Yes, Gary," I said, and lifted the bags.

"Then put your make-up back on."

"Uh-huh." I knew my role in the household this week.

"Then you can think about what you're going to make me for dinner."

Yes. All traditionally female tasks were mine.

He swatted my ass as I passed.

I was thankful the butt plug was no longer jammed up there.

I set the shopping bags on my bed, then fetched my mother's make-up. I'd worn so much of it this week I was beginning to worry she'd notice the difference when she got back. Then again, I probably had bigger problems to face when she got home. If Aunt Shauna was to tell her about the pornographic movies I'd supposedly bought, my mother might decide to hunt through my bedroom until she found them. Safely hiding my lingerie and toys wasn't going to be easy. In fact, it was proving nearly impossible. I temporarily stashed the bags at the bottom of my wardrobe.

I spent several minutes restoring myself to beauty in the bathroom, giving myself more of a bronzed glow than I'd done before. It was important to change things up. I had to keep my man interested, after all.

Until he went back to his wife.

I hated how he had a woman at home. His real home. Not this charade of a fantasy we were living out here.

I threw the thought to one side, then returned to my bedroom and stripped out of my clothes. Stood in just my red ribbon, I fetched the new leather skirt he'd bought me and slipped into it. It was incredible. A perfect fit. And just so fucking sexy.

My mobile beeped.

MY MOTHER – Why is Gary back in the house? Xxx

I froze. Had Aunt Shauna really told her already? But she'd only seen us together in the city. It was a bit of a leap – or a crossed-wire – to assume he was back here. And what of those X's? Were they truly reassuring or lulling me into a false sense of security? I decided to play it cool, neither lying about – nor denying – his whereabouts.

ME – What makes you say that? Xx

MY MOTHER – Betty saw you and him get out of our car. Stop dodging the question! And it'd be nice if you asked how our trip is going xxx

Despite the discomfort of having the butt plug still inside me throughout the journey, I was thankful Gary had let me drive home. Optics were everything for Betty, after all... The nosy, old hag.

ME – How's your trip? Have you seen plenty of the sights as you'd planned? I didn't want to say, but my computer was playing up again xx

I deliberately referred to the computer problems in the past tense, hoping she'd assume Gary had already left.

MY MOTHER – He's fixing it again? Oh dear, how are you going to pay him? xxx

She hadn't answered my questions about Germany. She didn't care to. And likely because her only interest was in what the hell was going on between Gary and I.

ME – It's okay. He says he won't take any more money xx

MY MOTHER – That's really nice of him. Well for goodness sake make sure you look after him! Xxx

My clitty stiffened under my skirt.

ME – I will xx

CHAPTER 19

I walked into the living room in my leather skirt and bra.

Gary was sat on the sofa.

"My mother just told me I have to look after you," I said quietly, then dropped to my knees in front of him. "A girl's got to do what she's told." I unzipped his fly, then wrestled his trousers to his ankles. "Oh, lover." I grabbed the outline of his cock through his boxers and rubbed up and down. "Will you promise me something?"

"Anything, Princess."

I hauled down his boxers. "Flood my mouth with your semen." I swallowed his shaft.

Gary grunted, as his head hit the roof of my mouth. He grabbed my hair in a bunch and began to face fuck me.

I felt so used. It was incredible. My clitty bobbed up and down as I motioned my mouth in unison with his strokes.

"Oh, I *am* going to make you swallow, baby."

I murmured my agreement, as his balls struck my chin. I couldn't believe how right it felt to suck this magnificent cock. I was born to do this. Destined to be on my knees pleasuring a man. I slurped a delicious mixture of saliva and precum, as that thought permeated my mind further. Would I ever need to find another man to do this to? If I never saw Gary again? I almost surrendered to tears as I momentarily gagged.

He slowed his motion.

"Don't!" I quipped, and threw my lips back down his length.

"Good girl, baby. You'll adapt, learn to breathe through your nostrils... Like the cocksucker you truly are."

Cocksucker! I loved it! I wanted him to write it all over my body, dress me up in tatty, tarty clothes adorned with the word and to make me never forget what I was now.

"*My* cocksucker, Princess."

I gargled on our juices, wishing I could entice ever more precum from his slit.

His face was reddening already.

I knew he wouldn't last long.

"I really enjoyed today."

I knew what part he enjoyed most.

"Torturing you, baby... *Humiliating* you."

I momentarily closed my eyes. I let his cock slip from between my lips. "I want to obey you."

He grinned.

I kissed the head of his prick as I made girly eyes up at him. "Without question."

He smiled further.

"But you must wait until tomorrow," I whispered, then sucked him all the way inside me.

Gary grunted like never before.

I hitched my leather skirt up at the rear, exposing my whole ass.

"You've no idea how much I want to fuck you there, Princess."

I devoted all my efforts to emptying his balls.

"To take your virginity..."

I knew I wanted it too.

"To take it home with me..."

Home.

"And have it as mine forever."

With his wife.

Gary reached over my head and smacked my bare behind.

I thundered my face into his pelvis, my chin to his sack and fed the tip of his phallus into my throat.

"Jesus, sissy!"

Oh my God! I loved it!

He grabbed hold of the back of my head and forced his cock

further into me. "Take it! Take it all! Take my fucking cum!"

And he was swearing at me too! I gagged. I almost choked.

Gary's cock swelled in my mouth.

My eyes bulged in my head.

He didn't care that I couldn't breathe.

And neither did I. Momentarily. I was on another plane of existence, where my needs – even my basic survival needs – no longer mattered.

Gary unleashed a hellacious howl. His fingers grasped my head harder.

I sensed it about to happen. I was in heaven.

His magnificent, unsheathed shaft erupted the first volley of semen into my throat.

I felt somehow unable to properly swallow. His cock was stopping my throat from functioning.

He spurted out a second shot.

I locked my lips tighter on him.

Gary hammered every inch of his hard-on into my mouth.

I could feel the incredible change in his testicles on my chin.

"Fuck, baby!" he cried out, as third, fourth, fifth, sixth and possibly even seventh and eighth loads launched from his length.

I could feel his cum starting to slide down my throat.

His fingers relented on my skull first, taking more sensually to my hair.

I tried in vain to channel my breathing through my nostrils.

Gary wheezed as he began to retreat his rod from my throat.

I gasped around it.

He patted the top of my head. "Good girl."

I tongued the underside of his cock.

He continued to pat me in the most patronising of fashions. "You can tell your mother you took real good care of me..."

I finally swallowed all the semen I could muster as he withdrew. Oh God, it was even more intense and exciting than I'd ever fantasised. I was his personal cum dump – eager, loyal and obedient.

"Definitely a daughter she can be proud of," he said, wiping his leftovers across my lips and giving my head a final pat.

"Sissy?" I asked, looking up from the floor to him. "You've never called me that before."

He let out a long exhalation, then said nothing.

Wasn't he going to explain? "Gary?"

"Didn't you like it?" he asked.

I hesitated. Why was I suspicious he'd been thinking of someone else? Some other clitty-owning, girly cum-slut like myself? "I... I loved it... Sir."

Gary smiled. "Sir? Oh, I like the sound of that."

I made a mental note for Wednesday... And hoped he had as well.

He pulled me up from my preferred position on my knees. "You *are* selfish, however, Princess."

I stood, my leather skirt up around my waist and my little clitty on display in my ribbon before him. "How am *I* selfish, Gary?"

He grinned as some of his cum slid from the corner of my lips. "Because you've eaten and I haven't."

My clitty pulsated. "Oh, Gary, you're amazing... The things you do to me with your words... I'll fetch your dinner for you now."

CHAPTER 20

My head was in a rush for the rest of the evening as I intimidated myself with fantasies about the following day, then quickly informed Gary when I thought of a ground rule over something I couldn't bare to be forced to do.

Each time followed a similar path.

"Really, Princess, are you sure you want to exclude this fun?"

I'd reluctantly nod, so terrified of disappointing him.

He'd agree to it, then treat me either with silence or indifference.

His only actual complement was on the dinner I made him. "More than adequate, sissy," he said.

My clitty almost tore my ribbon as she hardened under my skirt. "Anything else you were pleased with today, sir?" I asked, as he led me to the bedroom as the sun set.

He grunted.

"Sir?"

Gary said nothing.

I wanted desperately to be praised for being his cocksucker.

And he knew it.

I stopped by the bed as Gary undressed. "May I do anything else for you, sir?"

His response was almost a scowl.

I suspected I'd set too many ground rules for his liking. However, hadn't he realised the treasure I'd deliberately avoided? The absolute, most important thing of all? I'd refused to ground rule against it!

"You sleeping in those?" he said, hauling off his boxers and glancing at my skirt and bra.

I bit my lower lip. "I did say earlier that I couldn't wait to dress up for you tonight." I unzipped my skirt, then slipped it down my smooth legs. "I was thinking of the lingerie-"

"That can wait until tomorrow."

My bra was half-unhooked. I let it fall away regardless, so I was stood only in my red ribbon.

Gary got into my bed.

I felt almost boyishly naked as he stared at my body.

"You're desperate to dress up in your new items, sissy, aren't you?"

I nodded.

"You feel exposed, right?"

"Yes, sir," I whispered, fearing I was prematurely falling into the trappings of outright obedience.

"Does your ass feel empty?"

I inhaled, rather raggedly.

"Do you wish you still had the cucumber from the hotel?"

"I do, Gary- I mean, sir." I dared lean my knees on the edge of the bed. "Perhaps you'd like to try out the new dildo on me." I felt my sphincter expand as I thought of the bulging veins and bulbous head.

"Tomorrow," he snapped, then shoved my knees off the bed. "Unless you make another rule about that."

"I won't, sir. I've no more rules to make. I promise."

He looked at my ribbon.

I stood in awkward silence.

Gary leaned forward and untied it, then tossed it onto the floor.

I was completely naked in my own bedroom, my make-up and the last of my jewellery the only clue to my inner gender. "If not the dildo, sir, may I suggest you still have your fingers?"

"And my tongue, Princess."

My legs trembled with anticipation. "May I turn around for you, sir?"

He shook his head.

"You don't want to lick my hole?" I asked, my voice whiny

and full of despair.

"Not now."

I clasped my hands together. "*Please* may I be permitted to wear something for you?" Everything about my surroundings reminded me of my masculine upbringing. I was desperate to shed the bondage of my past – and of my parents.

"Get the nipple clamps, Princess."

"I can read your wonderful mind so easily, Princess," Gary said, tugging on the chain attached to my nipple clamps.

I tried to suppress my moans as I lay back beside him, snug on my single bed.

"Your past collides with you in this setting, doesn't it?"

I closed my eyes, suppressing both the emotional and physical pain. Then I tried to speak-

"Shush, sissy, no more ground rules... You promised."

I nodded.

He removed the last of my jewellery, then smeared sweat from his palms across my cheekbones and alongside my eyes. "I'm going to make your perspire- No, sweat so much, that I'm going to deny you the last of your femininity." He tried to rub out the last of my lipstick.

I focused momentarily on the colour on my fingernails.

"You chose this room, Princess. You didn't want me to fuck you in your parents' room... A room your mother has left with a definitive feminine touch."

I bit my bottom lip as he stretched my nipples further.

"You know how this would look to your Aunt Shauna, if she walked in right now?"

I wouldn't answer him. I wouldn't-

He tugged hard on the chain.

"Fuck- Sorry, sir."

"What're you sorry for?" he demanded. "For being a sissy? For being a princess?"

"For swearing," I said swiftly.

"Or for being Mark-"

"Don't-"

He stared me into silence.

I closed my eyes again.

"That's good, you're beginning to know your place. You have no identity at all. No desires. No needs. No say. It's not even Wednesday, and you're already surrendering everything to me."

"Yes, sir," I said, and cursed inwardly at how the femininity was beginning to escape my tone.

"Tell me what your Aunt Shauna would see if she walked in on us right now?" Gary said, then pulled the duvet off the bed completely.

"She'd see two men in bed, sir." I felt so ashamed. So humiliated. My face was tingling as it turned ever redder.

Gary placed my palm on his massive erection. "What's the younger one doing to the older one?"

I couldn't say it.

Gary emphasised his point with a sudden jerk of the chain, yanking my nipples so hard my back rose from the bed.

"He's making him hard, sir," I said, suppressing true tears.

"And what does that make the younger one?"

"He's a faggot, sir."

"*Who* is?"

I hated myself in that very moment. "I am. I'm a queer. I'm bent, fruity, gay... A faggot."

Gary throbbed in my hand.

Yet I wasn't even caressing him. I couldn't. I was frozen. Trapped in the midst of disgust and inner turmoil.

He released his hold of the chain.

I could focus only on the emotional trauma I was experiencing.

Until he pinched hold of my tiny, unaroused sex. "What would Aunt Shauna make of this? The younger one isn't enjoying it."

I didn't dare answer him.

"Why not?"

I gulped.

"Answer me."

"I don't know, sir–"

"Liar!"

We'd never role-played anything like this.

He made a mild attempt to wank me into life.

My limp dick wouldn't respond.

"Something's wrong with the younger one," Gary said. "The older one is fine." He deliberately motioned his girth between my fingers. "Aunt Shauna wouldn't miss that." Gary took my hand off his hard-on. "Touch your own."

I took hold of my measly excuse for a couple of inches.

"That isn't a cock, is it?"

"It's a very small one," I said quietly.

"It's a clit."

"But I thought–

"You're not a faggot, are you? You're not gay. You're not a poof, a bender, or any of those derogatory terms I've always promised you you're not. You're Princess. *My* Princess. *My* sissy. *My* cocksucker. And you, more than anything else, are *my* beautiful, stunning girl."

I hesitantly opened my eyes and looked at him.

He looked so very different now. Strong. Confident. Almost caring. "Masturbate her for me."

Her?

"Your clit, Princess. Make her cum." Gary took hold of his cock. "And I'll make myself cum at the same time."

I was almost powerless to move.

Gary grabbed the chain again, then yanked my chest into life. "Milk her, Princess."

I diligently went to work on her for him.

He repeatedly tugged at the chain to emphasise how hard I should make my efforts on my tiny sex.

"Oh God, sir," I gushed.

He twisted the chain for good measure, dragging my nipples painfully closer together. "Always remember who you truly are, Princess, regardless of what you're wearing or the room, or the great outdoors, in which you lie."

I furiously fisted around my clitty.

"Or the man who's buried his cock deep inside you."

Oh God.

"You're the girl. *Always*. No ifs, no buts."

"Yes, Gary, yes!"

"You'll need to remember all of this tomorrow... Because I'm going to take you to extremes you never thought possible."

I could no longer speak.

"I'm going to take your very..."

My virginity?

"Soul," he whispered.

I ejaculated into the air. "Gary!" It landed nearby on my bedsheets.

He flooded a huge area of the bed next to me, snarling loudly throughout his climax and clasping the chain tightly.

My nipples felt like there were going to wrench out from my chest. I cried out.

Gary let go of the chain.

I wheezed as the last of the orgasmic bliss left my body.

His mammoth member leaked yet more liquid.

"The sheets," I said, giggling. "They're covered in your cum-"

"*Our* cum," he corrected, as he unclasped my nipples from the clamps. "And I'll remind you that cleaning them tomorrow is still included in your traditional duties."

I nodded, the pain in my chest still extreme.

"Just because you'll be obeying my every sordid command doesn't mean you'll have an excuse to shirk your housework duties, sissy."

I beamed with glee. "Yes, sir!"

Gary reached over me and retrieved my bra. He started to put it on me.

"Gary, please, my nipples are too sore to wear that-"

"I don't care, you're wearing it."

I acquiesced to him in silence, and winced as the material cut against my sensitive nipples.

He sensually retied my red ribbon, kissing my inner thigh as he did, then he tossed me the leather skirt. "Wear this in your sleep too."

"Okay, Gary."

He lay back on the bed. "And remember, Princess, that the moment the new day begins you must offer me absolute obedience without question.

"Except for everything we agreed was forbidden," I insisted.

"Of course, Princess, but everything else is a go."

It was 23:00 as he pulled me over his cum on the sheets for a goodnight kiss.

"Night, Gary."

"Get a good rest... You'll need every precious minute."

I listened to him fall asleep within a couple of minutes. Yet I was nervous and found it difficult to get over. The clock kept ticking.

What was I letting myself in for?

Absolute obedience.

And then I eventually drifted off with my palm lovingly wrapped around his girth.

CHAPTER 21

The alarm on my bedside radio blasted suddenly.

What the fuck?

Gary's cock was still in my hand.

I twisted my body to check the time, peeling my side from Gary's cum stuck to the bedsheets.

"It's game time," Gary announced loudly.

I was shocked. The time was midnight.

He started to rise out of bed, pushing me onto my little feet.

I spun around, ready to tell him how early it was, that the alarm had gone off in error and that at most I'd only had 15 or 20 minutes sleep.

Gary's stern glance told me everything I needed to know.

This was no error. This was Wednesday. And the day of total obedience had begun.

"Gary-"

"Shush, sissy. You're only to refer to me as sir today." He stepped into his boxers. "You may return to calling me Gary on Thursday... If you find you've any free will left."

I shuddered.

"Pardon, sissy?"

"Yes, sir, how may I obey you?"

"Strip the bed, then strip yourself, cocksucker. You can leave the ribbon on, but nothing else."

I diligently set about my duties with the bed.

Gary slipped on his socks, then his shoes.

I knew better than to ask.

He slid a pair of red stilettos across the carpet to me. "Wear these."

I finished stripping the sheets, then stepped into the heels. "Would you like me to touch up my make-up or put on some jewellery for you?" I asked, as I slid down my skirt and slipped out of my bra. My nipples were still so sore.

"You're only to do what I tell you, sissy, understand?"

"Of course, sir."

"Good girl, now run along with the bed sheets to the garage."

"The garage, sir?" Like this? Now? But that would require me to venture outside, naked. I was so afraid of being seen by the neighbours, even if it was dark and late.

"Yes! Now, hurry up!"

I'd stupidly never thought to make a rule about any of this, so I didn't protest despite my better instincts.

He slapped my ass as I passed him. "Lose the attitude about your lack of sleep, Princess, you're decades younger than me."

"Sorry, sir," I said, although certain I'd shown no defiance at all to him. And I'd no intention to.

He followed me into the kitchen.

I hesitated at the back door.

"Take a deep breath, if you must, but no further stalling."

"Yes, sir," I said, then looked out through the glass to check that Jim and Betty's lights were out.

Gary reached past me, opened the back door and pushed me outside.

My heels clicked loudly as I steadied myself on the ground outside. I looked left. Their lights were, fortunately, all off.

Gary walked back across the kitchen floor.

My heart pounded as I quickly hurried off towards the outhouse at the garage.

Gary flicked on the outside light, revealing me in all my sissy, naked glory.

I stumbled on my stilettos as I sped up.

Gary followed behind me. "Take your time," he barked.

I was thankful he hadn't called me sissy out here.

"*Sissy.*"

I should've fucking known better than to expect small

mercies from him.

"What a glorious night."

I flung my fingers onto the door handle of the outhouse. It was fucking locked! I dared look over my shoulder.

Gary was right up against me in a second, pressing his clothed groin into my bare ass.

"It's locked," I whispered.

He began to grind himself against me.

"Do you have the key?"

He grunted as he grew harder.

"Please-"

"Were you *actually* about to make a request from me?" he demanded.

"No. No, of course not." I could hear a neighbour's television. "I live to obey you, sir."

Gary reached around my midriff, stroked my bare skin, then slid his fingers down to my soft clit. He fondled me without a response.

I stood in awkward silence, trying to find positivity in that his bigger body probably shielded me from sight if Jim or Betty were already spying through their many windows.

He breathed over my shoulder. "I bet you wish you'd made better rules."

I did. "I only wish to please you, sir."

He backed slightly away from me.

I dared look back, as he slipped his hand into his boxers. Oh my God, surely he wasn't going to make me suck it out here-

He pulled out the key to the outhouse, then placed it in my hand. "Go on."

I was shaking as I tried to unlock the door.

He laughed.

I finally opened it, and rushed inside.

Gary followed, then shut the door behind us. "What are you waiting for?"

I looked at his crotch.

"Not me, silly." He tutted. "Put the sheets in the washing

machine."

"Of course, sir," I said, then kneeled down to attend to my domestic duties.

"You sissies are all the same, all you think about is sex. Specifically, cock. Isn't that right, Princess?"

"Yes, sir."

"What are you, sissy?"

"A cocksucker, sir."

He smiled as he watched me load up the machine. "*My* cocksucker."

I nodded, then started the wash.

Gary looked down at me.

I opted to remain on my knees until he ordered me otherwise.

He just stared at me.

I felt so very naked, intimidated and yet sexy and alluring at the same time.

He kept gazing.

"Is something wrong, sir?"

He shook his head. "Not for me."

"Sir?"

"Things are about to get very intense for you, though. I hope you're ready, sissy."

I gulped.

"Look into the garage, Princess. You see the way your mother has a hanging rail she uses to dry her washing?"

"Yes, sir."

"You see the rope pulley system? Well, I want you to go into the garage now and stand next to the ropes that are tied around the metal hooks on the wall."

I felt trepidation as I took my first loud steps down into the garage.

"I'm sure you think your imagination tells you what's coming next..."

My clitty shrivelled.

"Trust me, Princess, it certainly does not."

CHAPTER 22

I stood with my legs apart and my back to the metal hooks on the garage wall.

"You're shaking, Princess," he said, stood in front of me and looking me up and down. "You're terrified, aren't you?"

I breathed deeply in. "I want to obey everything you ask of me, sir."

"*Everything?*"

I nodded.

"What, even the things you set ground rules against?"

I said nothing.

He ran his forefinger to my chin, forcing me to look him in the eye. "Speak freely, sissy."

I gulped. "You promised you'd respect the ground rules, sir. I don't want to ruin your day by reminding you-"

"Of course, I'll respect them. I'll adhere to them fully... Well, maybe I'll side-step them, at worst. But what I mean, sissy, is what do *you* want to do right now?"

"Obey you, sir, without hesitation."

He smiled. "You have, Princess." His girth was growing harder still in his boxers. "But, truthfully, what do you wish for, what do you yearn for, outside of obeying me? Tell me the truth, I'll know if you're lying."

"Well, sir... I wish I was still in bed... Sleeping."

"You're tired?"

"Yes, sir."

"You want more sleep?"

"Yes, sir, but I want to obey you more. I promised you this. I will do whatever it takes to please you for the next twenty-four hours."

He leaned forward and gently kissed my lips. "Good, sissy, I see no reason why we can't both get what we want in here."

I forced a smile as he backed away again. I looked over his shoulder at the long window behind him which looked onto the side of the other neighbours' house. Yes, it was just after midnight and the chances of anyone being out there at this time to look in was slim. But it wasn't impossible. The neighbours on the other side had an adjoining path with ours out there. If they had any reason to use that path they'd see us in here, especially with the light shining so brightly on us.

Gary walked around me and unhooked the ropes from the wall, lowering the hanging rail slowly into the middle of the garage. "You see, Princess, my darling, sissy slave, I recognise you're tired, maybe even exhausted, and you're definitely out of your comfort zone. Tying you up isn't even my deepest desire right now."

How was he going to tie me up? The rope was only part of a pulley system to raise and lower the hanging rail.

"It's just to stop you running, and in doing so ruining my fantasy."

"I swear I wouldn't run, sir."

"You might." He placed the ropes in my hands. "I'm removing that option. Now, hold those ropes steady so the rail hangs exactly where I've left it."

I was as confused as ever, and clung tightly to the ropes as I watched him inspect the hanging rail up close.

Then Gary retrieved several of my father's 1.5 litre containers of paint from a corner in the garage.

"What are you going to do to me, sir?"

He placed them beneath the hanging rail, then raised the handles.

"Sir?"

He shushed me, then tweaked both my nipples before he made his way up the steps to the outhouse.

I was wincing, the agony from the clamps still residually

strong on my chest.

Gary returned with thick balls of string. He started to tie the handles of each bucket of paint to the hanging rail.

"You're... Weighing the rail down?" I asked. "Why, all you need to do is wrap the ropes around the hooks on the wall? They're more than strong enough to keep the rail in place."

He grinning. "Oh, stupid girl, haven't you figured it out yet?"

"No, sir."

He took one of the ropes from me and began to wrap it around one of my ankles, then he tied it in the tightest of knots. He repeated the process on my other ankle.

"You're tying me up?" I asked.

He took another rope and proceeded to bind my wrists together. "Oh, sissy, so much more than that."

I gasped.

He grinned.

"What are you planning, sir? Please, we agreed no foreign objects! The ropes are foreign objects!"

"Sissy, you and I both know very well the rule about foreign objects only concerned penetrating you... Don't try to manipulate me again."

I hesitated. "Sorry, sir."

He tested the knots on my ankles and wrists. "These are secure. They'll hold you."

"Hold me? Hold me where?"

Gary took the fourth rope, which was linked to the other three via the pulley system, and stepped towards the hooks on the wall. He started to tug at the rope, stretching the other three. "I'm going to suspend you in mid-air, Princess."

"Suspend me?" My stilettos scuffed the ground as I felt my ankles start to lift off the ground. "What?" I felt like I was falling forward. "Why, Ga- Sir?" I started to tumble down.

"To clean you..."

The ropes held me mere feet off the ground. I was suspended, and powerless to move.

"... In the most humiliating manner I can think of."

I breathed heavily in and out as Gary raised me higher until I was just about the same level as his chest. I felt in such danger, knowing a fall from this height on such a hard surface, and with no way to put my hands out to protect myself, would definitely injure me.

He wrapped the rope around the hooks, then let go.

I remained trussed in place, horizontal and face down.

He checked the buckets of paint and the hanging rail. "Everything's holding, Princess, you're fine."

My legs were held wide open, and I'd no means to shut them; such was the strength of the ropes. "What if something snaps, sir?"

"It won't. I order you to trust me... Do you trust me?"

"Yes, sir," I lied, although I hoped I sounded convincing.

He stroked one of my calves. "I believe the sincerity in your voice. Now, tell me, Princess, you got a lot of cum on you yesterday evening and you didn't wash, do you feel dirty? Unfeminine?"

"I guess," I said reluctantly.

Gary began to unfurl the hosepipe by the wall and took hold of the handle of the nozzle, then he turned the tap – the only tap, the cold water tap – all the way it would go.

"Sir, it's the middle of the night, it's cool in here, you're not really-"

Gary pulled the trigger and sent a hard, high pressure jet of water forcefully over my suspended body.

I tried to suppress my squeals, but sheer terror struck me as the brute force of the water sent me swinging through the air.

He was laughing, almost demonically.

I swung helplessly to and fro.

Gary released the trigger.

Load after load of cold water trickled from my body to the ground below.

Gary approached me, grabbed my hair and pulled at it until I faced him. "That make-up has to come off. It's bad for your skin to sleep in it, sissy."

But I wasn't sleeping-

Gary blasted the cold water into my face.

I couldn't fight him off.

He held me firmly in place regardless. "Don't squirm, sissy."

I had to resist every physical instinct not to turn my face away.

He pointed the nozzle over my head and down my back. "Good girl, Princess, you'll be rewarded for that." He stroked my cheek with his free hand. "You're very brave, very special."

My spine and my buttocks were already shivering under the onslaught. When the water finally fell from my face and I could open my eyes again, I saw Gary's cock was sitting over the top of his boxers. I'd never seen him so erect. My suffering was his greatest arousal.

He took his finger off the trigger. "Are you clean now? I order you to tell me the truth, sissy."

"I am, sir, I promise I am. You didn't miss a spot. There's no cum on my body."

Gary walked around me, stroking my flesh. "You're clean everywhere?"

"Yes, sir."

He swatted my rear. "Clean everywhere *outside*, but what about inside?"

"Sir?"

He swatted me harder.

I was shaking both through fear and through the viciousness of the cold.

Gary shoved the nozzle against the entrance to my anus. "What about in here?"

"Sir, please, no!"

"Did I order you to beg me not to, Princess?"

"No, sir, I'm sorry. I didn't mean to-"

"Beg me to pull the trigger." He pushed it ever so slightly into the opening of my rectum. "Beg for it, sissy."

I was almost hyperventilating.

"Now!"

"Pull... The... Trigger... Sir-"

Gary fired a jet of water into my ass, propelling me forward and causing the most outrageous of sensations within my most fragile parts. He stopped seconds later, and I felt sheer shame as the water rushed right back out again, right in front of him. I looked down on the ground to see a tiny freckle of faeces slide down the sloping ground towards the garage door.

"Princess?" he asked. "Are you crying?"

I hadn't even realised. My emotions were beyond my control. I was almost broken.

"What are you crying for?"

I tried to sniffle in silence.

"That didn't hurt you, did it?"

Not physically, but how could I explain that to him?

Gary set down the nozzle and hose pipe.

I cursed myself for disappointing him.

He took my face in his hands and gently caressed me, sweeping my dripping wet hair from my eyes. "You're okay, I promise you, Princess."

"I... I'm sorry... I don't want to displease you. I don't want to let you down. I know how much this day, Obedience Day, means to you."

" Obedience Day," he said proudly. "I like the sound of that. What's wrong, did the water hurt your insides?"

I gave my head the merest of shakes. "It was just a shock to the system."

He stroked my skin. "Just breathe, Princess. I want to clean you. And I don't want you to run away, that's all."

"I won't."

Gary looked at the ropes, as if to suggest there was no chance of that happening anyway, but he said nothing. "Can you continue?"

He wanted to shoot water inside of me *again*? But surely it counted as a foreign object. He was breaking a ground rule. This whole Obedience Day should've been cancelled immediately. He'd forfeited the game. I needed to tell him. Even if it meant ruining what time we had left together.

He kissed my forehead. "I read this beautiful mind of yours so well. I know your fears. Shed them, baby. I'm giving you an enema. Every good sissy deserves one before she gets…"

What? Fucked? Was he finally going to fuck me?

"Some anal joy."

My eyes were locked on his. What particular anal joy? With the dildo? Or with his cock? I'd deliberately made no ground rule forbidding it. If he ordered me to take his cock inside me, I'd obey him… Diligently.

"*Can* you continue?"

I forced myself to nod.

He leaned his lips to mine and kissed them.

I tried to slide my tongue to find his.

Gary broke the kiss.

I sighed.

He moved around to my side, then reached down to retrieve the nozzle and hose pipe. He pointed it high in the air and pulled the trigger, sprinkling my entire body from my head to my arms, to my back to my bum and from my thighs to my feet in shivering, cold water.

I was truly drenched by the time he stopped.

"I order you to enjoy this experience, sissy."

"Yes, sir," I said, my teeth chattering and my eyes drawn again to the long window at the side. "Are… Are you enjoying it… Sir?"

His erection was so prominent and just – only just – still in my line of sight. "Some."

I felt water pool around my tiny clitty. My ribbon was a soaking mess.

Gary moved between my legs. "You look so pretty right now." He ran his fingers between my ass cheeks. "So vulnerable."

I anticipated him lowering the ropes, taking me down to his waist level.

He pointed the nozzle at my rear and shot another stream into me.

I was sent forward again by the force and shamed too when my innards inevitably dispelled the water out again.

Gary repeated the process.

I'd never felt so trapped, so controlled or so compromised. The blackness of the window lurked tellingly. There was little to no way of knowing if someone was outside, watching. The light of the garage showed only reflections. I felt endangered.

"I'm going to do it again, sissy, but this time I want you to try to hold it."

When he sent the next jet of cold water inside me, my internal muscles flinched as I flew forward and the water dribbled down onto the ground.

"Again."

I tried and failed a second time.

"Train your muscles, sissy. This is more than a game."

"I thought you were cleaning me-"

He slapped my ass and sent the longest volley of water up inside me yet. "Don't be cheeky, sissy, it's Obedience Day!"

As the water rushed out from me and my body steadied from swaying so much under a more constant flow, I started to clench.

Gary cut his grip on the trigger.

Some remaining water fell to the ground.

"We're going to do this all night until you learn, Princess."

I heard his fingers make contact with the trigger again. "Wait!"

"What is it?"

My teeth were steeled together. "I'm doing it, sir."

"You are?"

"Yes, I'm holding water." It felt like it was right up to my stomach.

He said nothing.

I felt like he was doubting me. Or, perhaps worse, studying me. Staring literally into my insides. I felt his breath on my cold bum.

"Relax your muscles, cocksucker."

My face reddened further as I obeyed my master, and

released the water from my innards to the ground below.

"Wow," he said. "You are amazing, Princess."

"Thank you, sir–"

He planted his face between my buttocks.

I elicited a squeal as I welcomed the warmth of his tongue on my sphincter, and tried to relax my muscles further to welcome him.

Gary delved his tongue deeper.

"Oh God," I quipped, without will. I'd wanted this so much only hours earlier, when he'd spurned my request. "Yes, sir, that's beautiful."

He withdrew his tongue. "I order your silence, sissy... We don't want to wake the neighbours."

I gulped, my mind crisscrossed by his hypocrisy.

Gary grazed his stubble against the smooth flesh of my rear, then lapped at my anus again. His tongue felt wonderful.

I hoped I tasted good.

The ropes creaked.

My little clitty stirred.

Gary twisted his tongue inside me.

My anus involuntarily contracted around it, as my wrists and ankles remained bound in place.

His fingertips made contact with my she-testes.

My clit elongated.

He rubbed my scrotum.

My ass craved a deeper, warmer lick.

Gary seemed intent to oblige, and prised my ring further open.

Moistness trickled from my body to the ground. I was still shivering, yet the sensations in my ass were heavenly. As if all the suffering of being trussed up and violated with harsh jets of water were worth it.

Gary stroked from the underside of my she-balls up higher.

I failed to contain a sneeze.

His fingertips were within touching distance of my clit.

I wanted so badly to be touched there. I had a raging she-erection.

He returned his fingers to the middle of my scrotum.

I wanted to arch my back to encourage his tongue deeper, but my bondage made such movement impossible.

He loudly ate at my asshole, the sounds reverberating off the brick walls of the garage.

My movements, so minimal, didn't even amount to a squirm, and the muffles from my mouth were suppressed to almost silence by my devotion to outright, unquestioned obedience. Yet, still my sex craved more. I could feel precum building beneath my foreskin. I was so turned on. My sex was rigid.

Gary tenderly took hold of my she-testes and gave them a gentle squeeze.

Pleasure pirouetted from my back passage to my she-penis. Somehow, I jolted and my soaking, red ribbon ripped.

Gary inhaled the aroma of my ass.

My ribbon fell, torn, to the ground below.

My lover took gentle hold of my naked sex.

I groaned.

He rapidly fired his tongue in and out of my anus. He was literally face-fucking me.

My body swung back and forth on the ropes in unison.

There was the sound of a twang from one of the strings tied around the paint buckets.

I wanted to propel my clit in his palm, but I didn't have the physical strength to overcome my restraints. My body was nothing but a vessel to his whims.

He stopped, and waited for my rear to swing back to him. He kissed my rectum.

I swung forward again.

He kissed it again upon my return.

My sex was desperate for release – for any sensual touch at all – but he just followed her with his palm. Never closing tightly. Never moving up and down on her. Just encasing her from the cool air of the garage.

His face was too far for another kiss on my next swing.

I needed more of that tongue.

He exhaled warm breath over my flesh, invigorating goosebumps on my rear.

I finally ground to a halt.

Gary remained motionless.

I was still and silent.

So was he.

Were we locked in a stalemate?

He offered no clues.

I knew I couldn't make a sound, nor a movement. This was his day.

He slowly removed his hand from my she-penis.

Was this it? Was he going to fuck me? I felt my sphincter pucker.

"You're a good girl, sissy." He patted my right buttock. "You've made me proud."

I wanted to thank him.

He stood up. "I told you we can both get what we wish for, so long as you obey me."

I almost understood.

He walked up the steps to the outhouse. "Do you want the light left on?"

I now understood.

"Or would you prefer to sleep in the dark?"

I hung painfully in mid-air, my limbs sore from the suspension, facing down at the wet ground. I was exhausted from both the onslaught and the sleep deprivation.

"You may speak, Princess. Light on or off?"

I ran the tip of my tongue across water on my lips. "Off please, sir."

Gary flicked the light switch off. "Sweet dreams." He stepped out of the outhouse and closed the door behind him.

I listened, waiting to hear him turn the key in the lock.

He didn't.

CHAPTER 23

My body hung lifelessly in the dark. The occasional drip of water from my skin was the only sound.

But inside my head was like a cacophony of banging drums. I felt nothing short of outrage that Gary had left me here like this. How the hell was I supposed to have the sort of sordid imagination which could've set a ground rule against this? It was beyond anything I'd ever expected of him.

I felt totally abandoned, as if I simply didn't matter to him. He hadn't pleasured my sex – still raging hard despite everything. He hadn't had sex with me. He hadn't even used my mouth on that mammoth tool of his. I'd seen how gargantuan my plight had made him. I felt both frustration and disappointment. He made my body and my mind go to a civil war within.

He'd just soaked and soaked me over and over, forcing my mascara to run, my lipstick to smear and the last of my self-esteem to disappear into some dark recess of the garage.

I was humiliated. Tied up and cast out of my own home. My parents' home.

I looked down at my torn red ribbon, coiled up on the ground in a puddle of water.

Liquid seeped from the corners of my eyes. I knew it hadn't come from the hosepipe.

I heard footsteps.

They were coming from outside. From the rear of the house. They were getting closer.

The handle to the outhouse turned. The door opened. Someone stepped inside.

I breathed silently, terrified to say a word in case I was alerting someone other than Gary to my presence.

The light flicked on.

My eyes were immediately sensitive, even though it'd only been a matter of three or four minutes since he'd left.

"You look beautiful, Princess," he said, then started down the steps. He set something on top of the freezer, then approached me with a towel. "Let me dry you. I don't want you getting sick."

My body involuntarily winced as he first touched me.

"You're okay, baby."

Baby!?!

Gary tenderly wiped the last remnants of water from all over my body, taking particular time between my buttocks and around my groin. "She's in some form tonight," he said, flicking my she-cock to and fro.

I said nothing.

"You're mad at me, aren't you?"

How could I answer? Who was I supposed to be? Baby? Princess? Sissy? Cocksucker? Slave? Had the fantasy finished the moment he walked out the door? When did I know when I was allowed to speak freely?

He rustled my hair with the same towel. "You're great at this role. I know you're angry. *You* know you're angry. But you're not permitted to say. You make for the most perfect submissive, you really do."

"I can't believe you left me here," I whispered, looking at the outline of his semi in his boxers.

"I was bluffing, Princess. I'd no intention of leaving you. I just needed to go to the toilet and get you a towel and some blankets."

I looked to what he'd set on top of the freezer. Blankets.

He moved back to my ankles and started to untie one of them. "And there's no way you're sleeping out here on your own. I just wanted to break you into your role. Big style. Think of it as a test, which you passed with flying colours. You're coming inside with me to sleep in a big, warm bed."

I was able to lower one stiletto-heeled foot onto the ground.

"Easy does it, baby." He untied my other ankle, helped me onto both feet and then unbound my wrists, kissing them softly. He glanced at my ribbon on the ground. "Shame." Then he looked at the buckets of paint weighing down the hanging rail. "I'll put that all away in the morning. Think of it as a man's task. You'll be preparing lunch, or putting a wash on... Or fixing your make-up." He looked at my face. "Sorry, you're such a mess." He ran the back of his hand across my cheek. "But *my* beautiful, sissy mess."

I coughed.

Gary ran to the blankets, grabbed them and quickly wrapped all three around me. "Let's get you to bed," he said, and scooped me up in his strong arms. "Even the most brutal of masters must tend to his slave's health. You'll not be getting hypothermia on my watch, Princess."

"Thank you, sir," I mustered.

He kissed my mouth. "Let's go."

I was carried up the steps to the outhouse.

Gary switched off the light, then carried me in my blanket and heels along the path at the rear of the house to the back door and into the kitchen. "You need a good sleep before the rest of Obedience Day."

I expected him to set me down, but he kept carrying me, looking me straight in my eye the whole time, through the kitchen, into the hall and up towards my bedroom.

He halted outside it. "You made the ground rules," he said, and carried me into my parents' bedroom.

I looked down to see the duvet already pulled back. "What are you doing?"

He set me down in my parents' bed.

"You can't do this!"

Gary threw the duvet over me.

"Not here!"

"Oh, shut up, Princess, did you make a rule against this? No, you didn't. So deal with it-"

"Deal with it?" I demanded. I was prepared not only to break character, but to break Obedience Day altogether.

He kicked off his socks and shoes, then tugged down his boxers. "Do you really want to be a whiny, little virgin all your life?"

I couldn't control my eyes from lighting up. Was this it? Was he finally going to order me to let him fuck me?

His hand grazed his cock. "Well?"

"No, sir," I said quietly, sinking into my submissive skin.

"Good," he snapped, and walked confidently naked around the bed to my mother's side. He got in beside me. "Cuddle onto me, sissy."

I rolled immediately onto my side and snuggled up against my master. "I'm sorry, sir."

"I forgive you." He kissed my lips.

I looked desperately into the depths of his eyes. "Do you want to-"

"Goodnight, Princess." He reached behind himself, switched off my mother's bedside light and shrouded the room in darkness.

I waited for his touch.

For his command.

And for my own tumultuous obedience.

CHAPTER 24

I was still a virgin when I awoke on Wednesday Morning, my eyes opening in horror at the reality of an older, naked man lying in my parents' bed. And myself alongside him.

I was so warm. I realised I'd perspired in my sleep, so I cast off my blankets, tossing them to the floor beside me. I was naked too. Shame overwhelmed me as I looked at the walls of the room. If my parents had even the slightest suspicion about this, my life wouldn't be worth living.

When I turned around again, Gary was awake and staring at me.

"Happy Obedience Day, sissy."

"Happy Obedience Day, sir."

He gave me a warm smile. "Did you sleep well, my Princess?"

"I did... Surprisingly." I ran my palm over the moisture on my chest. "I was too warm, though. I really need to get a shower-"

Gary pulled me into a loving embrace, running one hand through my hair and the other over my ass. He slipped his tongue into my mouth.

I was appalled, but I knew I had to comply. I started to kiss him back.

His member was soft.

So was mine.

Our sexes touched. Then seemed to somehow join. Gary's was obviously the more dominant one. Not just in its sheer size, length and girth, but in how it languished atop mine.

He pulled at one of my buttocks, then slid his fingers towards my hole.

My eyes opened as he, rather forcefully, dipped two of his

fingertips inside.

He was looking into my head. Through my eyes. Deeper.

I'm going to take your very soul.

"Get it on with me," he said, breaking his lips from mine.

"Here?" I asked, trying to mask my disgust with an innocence to my tone.

He stared at me, his cock already growing over mine.

"Are you ordering me, sir?"

"What did you expect, baby? You deliberately opted not to put a ban on full sex when you set your precious ground rules, isn't that right?"

I refused to concede to a nod.

He probed my rectum with his fingers. "You must want this, no?"

I whimpered.

"You were so meticulous when it came to your ground rules, sissy. *Why* did you not set one about this?"

I could feel it in my gut. I was about to get fucked. I wouldn't stop him. I couldn't. I'd set myself up for this.

Gary carefully lay me on my back, his fingers remaining inside me and his bulging cock over my crotch.

"Are you going to do it?" I asked. "Are you going to have sex with me?"

He manipulated my rear, bending his fingers in my rectum.

I cried lustfully out, my desires defying the taboo surroundings. My fingernails took to his back, dragging downwards.

He growled as he slid his cock up and down against my clitty.

My eyes widened as I felt her begin to grow.

Gary moved his other hand to my chin, clutching it and holding my face still. He drove his tongue into my mouth again, wildly demonstrating his dominance.

I submitted, as I knew I should, and meekly returned his kiss. I gently raised my rump, meeting the strokes of his sex with my own and clenching my sphincter on his digits.

He devoured me with every moving part of him.

I was there to be deflowered. Dissected. And destroyed.

Gary swirled my tongue around my own mouth. He pinned my clit against my own she-testes. And he made my anus open to my own wanton needs.

I winced as he added a third finger, then surrendered to the waves of pleasure which followed.

Order me, I said in my head, as I stared up into his powerful eyes.

He was so domineering in his touch and in his returning glare.

Order me to let you fuck me.

His eyes narrowed, as if somehow he truly could read my thoughts.

Order me to-

Gary flipped me over underneath him, twisting his fingers inside me so they never left me.

I panted as he more vigorously finger-fucked my hole and held me down so my sex was suppressed.

"You were made for Obedience Day, weren't you, sissy?"

"Yes, sir," I croaked, surrendering to my shame, and indeed almost inspired by the sacredness of my surroundings.

"You know where you are, Princess, don't you?"

"Yes."

"Where you never thought you'd be."

"No, sir."

"Not like this, sissy, not in your wildest dreams."

My rectum squelched under his pummelling. "Never, sir." Not ever.

"If I ordered you to speak freely, would you tell me to stop?" he asked, releasing his firm hold on my body and rubbing my skin.

I shook my head.

"Good girl."

I knew it was coming. I knew this was to be my moment. The moment I'd fantasised about, so secretly, for years. I was truly going to lose my virginity to this man. This man I was completely in awe of, and who I'd literally do anything for.

"I want to fuck you so much, sissy," he said, running his free palm from the small of my back all the way up to the top of my spine.

I slowly raised my rear, freeing my trapped clitty from the mattress. I spread out my arms and grabbed the sheets with my fingertips, knowing the penetration of his fingers would be nothing in comparison to the feel of his cock. "Order me," I whispered.

Gary's breathing was rapid.

My own frantic.

"That's enough," he said finally.

What?

He caressed my shoulder.

What did he mean by-

He withdrew the fingers of his other hand from my rear.

I panted, waiting in anticipation of what was supposed to inevitably come next.

"You truly are incredible, Princess."

My sphincter was puckering. I could feel it. I could *hear* it. My body was crying out for his cock!

"We're done here, sissy."

No!

"Take yourself off to the bathroom."

No! No! No!

"Shower."

No, this couldn't be!

"Then put your make-up on."

What had I done wrong?

"And dress up in what I leave out for you."

"Sir, please, I-"

"Silence, sissy!" he snapped. "Don't question my orders. This is *my* day. You're just a guest in it. Understood?"

I dragged my naked body across the bed. "Yes, sir," I said, and planted my feet on the floor. "And then?" Then would he fuck me, when I was at my most feminine, presentable best?

He grabbed hold of my arm, spinning me around to face him. "And make yourself convincing, Princess."

Convincing? When had I ever *not* been convincing to him?

"Because we're going for a drive." He stood alongside me, towering above as he looked down on me.

"What?" I demanded.

"We're going out together. We've somewhere to be. You're going there dressed as the most convincing, sexiest girl I've ever laid eyes on. And I don't want to be the only man there who sees it."

I was speechless. This wasn't on. This couldn't happen. This-

"After all, baby, there's no rules against it," he said, and walked out of my parents' bedroom and into mine.

CHAPTER 25

I'd finished my shower and applied my most *convincing* of make-up attempts so far when I finally unlocked the bathroom door and strutted out naked to the hall.

"Wow, baby, you look like a bloody goddess," Gary said, fully dressed and sat on the edge of my bed, gazing at me as I entered the room.

"Thank you, sir," I said firmly, ignoring the imagery in the corner of my eye of the clothes he'd laid out for me.

"What d'you think you're doing now?"

I bent right over to retrieve my mobile phone from the floor, then decided to stay in that position as I checked my messages.

"Sissy, I asked you a question."

"We agreed I could reply to my mother's texts."

Gary sighed.

I ignored him.

MY MOTHER – Your father took ill last night. I think it's food poisoning. He's very, very sick. He wants to see a doctor, so I know it's serious as you know your father. He has to be dying to go see one. BTW I got some weird texts from your Aunt Shauna xxx

Shit. Double shit.

I glanced behind me.

Gary was staring at my ass.

I stood up straight.

"I order you to make this mother and daughter reunion brief, sissy."

ME – What do you mean weird texts? Xx

My heart was pounding. Had Aunt Shauna ratted me out about the Ann Summers' bags?

MY MOTHER – I think Shauna has been drinking again. And so nice of you to show concern for your father! I swear to God when I get home you and I are going to have a long talk about your attitude lately. I hope you're keeping on top of your washing and the house is tidy because the last thing I want to come back to is your washing on top of mine and your father's. Have a nice day. We won't. This has been the holiday from hell. We are never going away again! xxx

Oh fuck.

Gary swiped the mobile out of my hand.

"Gary!" I cried, trying in vain to reach for it.

He smacked my ass hard. "I told you not to call me that today, you stupid sissy!"

"I need my phone, sir. It's my mother. Aunt Shauna sent her some weird texts and-"

"I don't care," he snapped. "If your mother bought the lies her sister was selling she'd have called you by now. She hasn't, so forget about it."

I glared at him.

Gary tucked my mobile into the pocket of his jeans. "You'll get it back in exchange for good behaviour."

"Sir, please, one of the ground rules was if my mother texts, you can't interfere. I'm supposed to be able to answer her. You're controlling that now, and it's wrong."

"You've answered her texts, haven't you?" he demanded.

I reluctantly nodded.

"Then I'm not interfering. And I order you to shut up about it."

I hesitated, then forced a smile. "Okay, lover." Although my sincerity was barely skin deep. "What have you picked out for me to wear?" My heart beat faster again as I thought of leaving the house dressed in-

"That sexy leather skirt, tight top, the crotchless red panties, red stilettos and…"

I gulped. "The butt plug." Hadn't he had enough fun torturing me with it yesterday?

"Ready to be inserted in your perfect, little asshole, Princess."

I was in no rush to leave the house, but I'd been naked around him long enough on this so-called Obedience Day already, so I stepped into the crotchless panties and pulled them up tight on my ass, leaving my clitty dangling between the gap in the lace. "Where are we going today, sir?"

"You'll see, sissy."

"Are you *actually* going to make me go for a walk in these?" I asked, slipping into the stilettos.

"We're not going for a walk. I told you already, Princess, I want to show you off to other men."

Other men? I found myself getting increasingly paranoid about just who these other men might be.

"Anyway, I'll let you finish getting dressed on your own. You look stunning. I'll go out and tidy the garage-"

I touched his arm. "Please, don't let the neighbours see you."

He looked me up and down like I was the stupidest whore he'd ever met in his life. "You're worried about the neighbours seeing *me*?"

I swallowed.

"I'll reverse the car into the garage, Princess. I'll pick you up in there, make it easier for you to sneak out without the rest of the neighbours seeing you."

"Thank you," I said, sounding even dumber than before.

He pinched my bum. "Just take quiet steps on your way from the back door to the outhouse." He giggled. "Something tells me Jim and Betty are a bit on the nosy side, but hey that's just an inkling… I could be totally wrong."

Was it wrong to want to call my lover an asshole to his face?

"I really wish you'd tell me where we're going," I said, my legs crossed in the passenger seat as Gary drove into town.

It was a bright, beautiful day and, even though I had the sun visor down, I felt as if every single person on the streets was staring into the car at me, like they knew what type of girl I really was – a fraud.

"I'm a nervous wreck, sir."

"Don't be, Princess. I promise you'll enjoy yourself. I'm doing this as much for you as for myself. You'll thank me afterwards, when you see how easy it is."

I held my palms up. I was visibly shaking.

"Trust me, if anything goes wrong, this'll hurt me more than it'll hurt you."

Jesus, did he *have* to talk like my mother?

"Uncross your legs, sissy."

I hesitated, then obeyed.

"Part them wider."

Despite a bus alongside us, I opened them. I shielded my face with my left hand.

"Good cocksucker," he said.

I anticipated his hand reaching across, slipping between my thighs and fondling my sex under my skirt.

He drove on without making a move.

My clitty languished outside the gap in my panties, almost frustrated at his lack of attention. I told myself to be grateful and to be careful what I wished for.

"Something wrong?"

"No, sir."

"You sure? I heard you sigh."

I had?

"Or was it a moan? Are you secretly enjoying yourself, Princess?"

I wasn't sure. "Maybe." No! I shouldn't have said that. Then I waited to see if he'd try to check.

His hands didn't leave the steering wheel, although his eyes diligently checked a street sign. He was looking for somewhere in particular.

I couldn't tell where, though. "Why are my legs open, sir?"

He ignored me.

"Are you going to touch me?"

He drummed the steering wheel.

"Are you going to make her hard?"

He clicked his teeth.

I couldn't take it anymore. I had to ask him outright. "Why didn't you fuck me this morning?"

"Knock that bad language on the head, slut," he said. "That's an order."

"Yes, sir. Sorry, sir."

Gary cleared his throat. "I went through your phone while you were getting ready."

"What? That's such an invasion of privacy... Er, sir."

His eyes were off the road, staring into me.

"Sir, the road?"

His pupils burrowed into my soul.

"Sir?"

"Sissy slaves have no right to privacy," he said, and finally returned his attention to the busy road ahead. "The relationship between you and your mother is toxic. She treats you like a child. And you act like one. It's embarrassing."

My face turned crimson to match my panties and heels, and my clitty shrivelled under my skirt.

"I don't think you're going to be truly capable of standing up to her until you lose your virginity. It'll change you for the good. You'll feel like an adult. And you won't take so much crap from her."

I couldn't hide my smile. I knew what he meant. He was definitely going to fuck me today. "I'm so excited," I said quietly.

"You're missing the point."

I was?

"Here we are," Gary said, and indicated to turn into the parking area of a shopping centre.

"The mall? Are you crazy? You really expect me to go in there, in front of all those people, dressed like this?"

"Expect, Princess?" He grinned. "I order it."

CHAPTER 26

Gary switched off the engine.

I crossed my legs and tried to compose my breathing. "Okay, wait. Don't open the door... Yet. I don't want to let you down-"

"You *can't*, Princess."

"Okay, you called me Princess. That's good." I looked him right in the eye. "I'm addressing you as sir, but I'm pleading to Gary within... The man I fell for online-"

"You fell for me?"

"Big style, sir. You know I have. Look at me. Look how far I've come. I don't know what you've planned for today. I know you want to parade me around the mall and have men look at me-"

"Lust for you, Princess."

My heart was pounding. "Sir, what if they can tell?"

"Tell what?"

"That I'm not a real girl!"

He reached his palm to my knee. "Baby, you are every bit a real girl in every way that matters. I want you to know that."

I tried to nod, but deep down I didn't believe it.

There were a group of girls around my age walking by the front of the car. They were scantily-clad, soaking up the sunshine. Smiling, laughing and enjoying life. They were the types men would lust after.

Not me.

"I want you to do this," Gary said.

I wondered if he'd use the remote, trigger the butt plug inside me and cause me colossal anguish and embarrassment the moment I set foot in the mall.

"Look up, Princess, tell me what you see."

I threw my eyes upwards to the outside of the building. "Bricks," I said.

"What else?"

"A billboard, sir."

"And what's on the billboard, Princess?"

I giggled. "Shrek."

"You mentioned it last week in an e-mail. You said you wanted to see it, but you'd no one to go with. Well, Princess, you do now."

I narrowed my eyes on him. "We're going to see a film?"

He nodded.

"We'll be sat in the dark?"

"Yes, baby, all you have to do is summon the courage to make the short walk from here."

I glanced to the entrance to the mall. "I've been here before, lover. The cinema's on the second floor."

"That's not far."

I let out a long exhalation, wanting to do it but fearing the consequences. "There's an escalator we have to go up."

"I can see it, sissy."

"My skirt, sir. It's so short. And my panties are crotchless."

Gary groaned with desire.

"This means a lot to you, doesn't it?"

He smiled. "Princess, to walk in there in front of people with you... I'll be the proudest man in this city."

I nodded. "Do you think people will know?"

He leaned forward and pecked my lips. "I don't think so, but even if they do I want them to know you're mine. And I'm not going to let anyone hurt you. I promise you that."

I looked again to the mall. "Okay, sir. I'm as ready as I'll ever be. Let's go."

We shut the car doors in unison.

I felt a gentle breeze at my bare legs.

Gary walked around the front of the car, then beckoned me to join him.

My legs were like jelly and my feet so awkward on my stilettos. I felt stupid. This was so different to being at home when it was just him and I. This was public. It was intimidating. It was frightening. It was beyond overwhelming.

Gary took my hand, giving a reassuring squeeze, then led me towards the front of the mall.

I saw a man looking at me from the inside of his car.

"That turns me on so much," Gary said.

"What does?"

"Knowing he wants to fuck my sissy."

I felt my sphincter tighten on my butt plug.

The automatic doors at the front of the mall slid open.

I could feel my clitty flipping and flopping under my skirt.

A mixed gendered group of people my age walked out.

Fearful I could know any one of them, I lowered my head as we entered. My bare flesh immediately reacted to the air-conditioning. Goosebumps dotted my skin.

Gary tried to reach for my hand. "Take it," he insisted, and led me towards the escalator.

I could feel perspiration everywhere from the inside of my bra to the crotchless sides of my panties.

Gary's hand tightened on mine. "Good girl."

My palm felt clammy within his.

He stepped onto the escalator first.

I felt an immediate moment of panic, uncertain where to set my feet and fearful of my heels becoming lodged in the grooves of each step.

Gary helped me on, then released my hand and transferred his touch to my rear, holding my buttocks through the leather of my skirt as we ascended.

I was stood with my legs tight together, scared even to look behind me in case someone was trying to look up my skirt.

Gary fondled my ass.

"Stop it," I whispered.

"No."

I pursed my lips.

"It's *my* day, sissy," he said, and slipped his fingertips under the end of my skirt.

I gulped as I felt his fingers make contact with the top of my thighs.

This had to be one of the highest escalators in the city. It just seemed to go on and on. It was certainly proving to be the longest journey I'd ever taken on one.

Gary pressed his fingers into the bottom of my buttocks.

I was blushing beyond belief.

He concentrated his touch between my cheeks.

I felt him put pressure on the butt plug. My pulse rate increased. And my sex jolted. "I could murder you," I said quietly.

"I order you not to." He was smiling. "No homicide today, Princess."

I heard giggling close behind us.

The next level of the mall started to come into view. It was much quieter than the ground floor, and the cinema was only a short stroll away. But it was a stroll I'd have to take again on my loud, clicking stilettos.

Gary let me walk off first.

I almost stumbled as I set my first foot on solid ground.

Gary steadied me by my ass.

"You're incorrigible," I said gently.

He put his hand into his pocket.

I was momentarily fearful he was going to switch the butt plug to vibrate.

He checked my mobile instead.

"Anything?" I asked.

He shook his head, and put it back in his pocket.

I guessed my efforts so far didn't qualify for good behaviour.

He handed me a five pound note. "I'll get the tickets, you get the popcorn."

"But-"

"Then we'll meet up and walk in together," he said, leaving me standing alone.

I joined the queue for the kiosk. It was busier and longer than

I expected for the time of day. I hated waiting, especially on my own. I dared not make eye contact with anyone. But I could feel the eyes of others on me. Could they tell? Or were they merely judging my slutty dress sense?

The queue moved quickly. Before I knew it, I was next in line.

I listened to the conversation of the customer ahead with the teller. Fuck, how was I going to speak? I could put on a girly voice for Gary, but how was I going to speak to a stranger? I couldn't very well use my real voice. But what would the reaction be to my-

"Next," said the male teller.

I timidly approached the till. "Popcorn, please," I said quietly.

"Sweet or salted?"

"She's always sweet," Gary said, appearing alongside me.

The teller looked between us, his eyes lingering a split-second longer on me. "Of course."

I drove my elbow into Gary's arm the moment the teller turned away.

"I got the tickets, but the movie doesn't start for another twenty minutes..."

"Okay," I said.

"Whatever will we do to entertain ourselves for twenty minutes?"

The teller set the popcorn on the counter.

I handed him the money.

He seemed to study my fingernails for more than a moment, before returning my change.

Gary led me away from the kiosk and towards the stairs up to the various screens. "Yeah," he said. "Him too."

"Him too what?" I demanded.

"He wants to fuck my sissy as well."

CHAPTER 27

"Look at this," Gary said, as we walked into the cinema to take our seats. "We're the only two people here." He had the widest grin. "Will you cosy up to me in the back row?"

"Yes, sir," I said, already certain of what was to come.

He swatted my ass as I stepped up the stairs in front of him.

The butt plug twisted within my tush.

"Go right to the end of the row, baby."

Right in the corner. Out of sight. I carefully sat myself down, then took several seconds of readjusting before I felt comfortable. I crossed my legs, stretching my sphincter around the plug and letting my clitty fall between my thighs.

Gary slipped one arm around me, then he took one piece of popcorn with his free hand. "Take this from me," he said, and placed it between his teeth.

"What?"

He leaned his lips towards mine.

Oh fuck. The lights were still up. There were bound to be security cameras recording us.

He planted his lips on mine.

I quickly took the popcorn from him, turned away and chewed.

"You're still trembling," he said. "Relax, sissy."

"I'm not trembling," I lied. "I'm just finding my way into this new environment at my own pace."

He shoved his hand into his pocket and tapped the first setting on the remote, sending vibrations into my anus. "Every time you lie to me, I'm going to increase the setting."

I touched his wrist, and squeezed. "Sir, please, it's so quiet in here." The plug inched out towards my entrance. "The moment anyone walks in, they'll hear it."

He flicked his eyebrows up and down, as if to suggest he couldn't have cared less.

The doors swung open.

My eyes widened. "Sir, please!"

"Give me a kiss."

I hesitated.

"Make it quick, before they can see–"

I don't know where I found the strength, but I practically pounced on my lover, shoving my tongue into his mouth and swirling it around for several seconds. I broke it a millisecond before another couple came into view.

The girl looked up regardless.

"I'll give you that one," Gary said, reaching into his pocket and switching off the vibrations.

I rested my forefinger on his knee. "Speaking of which, exactly *when* are you going to give me one?"

The couple sat several rows in front of us.

"Maybe we'll see how busy it gets in here first, sissy."

"You wouldn't, would you?"

He smiled.

"You'd actually order me to... Y'know... Here?"

"Order you to what, Princess?"

I realised I could just about overhear the conversation between the other couple in front, and immediately lowered my voice. "Let you fuck me?"

He grabbed my leg and forcefully uncrossed it from the other. "Spread them wide, sissy," he said, quietly.

I felt both threatened and reassured. He wanted to have fun with me in this setting, but he also wanted to be subtle. He'd no wish to be overheard either.

Gary slipped his hand underneath my skirt and pinched hold of my sex with his forefinger and thumb. "Mmmmmm, she's so small." He rotated his thumb over the head, rubbing hard on my slit.

"Sir, it's too bright in here for that. There's security cameras. We'll get caught. We'll get thrown out."

The curtain on the big screen began to draw to either side.

The doors opened, and more people filtered in.

The lights began to dim.

Gary gently masturbated me. "You were saying, Princess?"

I couldn't help smiling at him. The trailers. Of course.

He watched where the other people sat as he pulled at my sex, elongating her. "I order you to enjoy this."

The pleasure in my she-penis and the awkwardness of the slightly dislodged butt plug was already causing my back to arch. "Yes, sir," I said, breathlessly.

He wrapped his other arm around my neck and dragged me into a kiss, roughly striking my tongue with his own and refusing to break for air. He thundered his forefinger and thumb on my clit.

The dramatic sound of another trailer starting drowned us out.

My fingers went instinctively for the bulge in his jeans. "Sir." I watched people take their seats in the rows in front of us. They were getting closer. It was only a matter of time before somebody tried to sit in the same row of us. "Be careful."

His palm flew around my little length, holding all of her in one clasp.

I couldn't help myself, gyrating into his touch. I was losing my senses.

"Are you enjoying this, sissy?"

I bit my lower lip, then conceded a nod as I groped the outline of his cock.

"The danger's turning you on?"

"Yeah." I was shedding yet more inhibitions, rocking my ring on the butt plug against the seat. "Switch it back on, sir, please."

Gary obliged.

I felt the infiltration in my anus amplify.

His touch on my sex exorcised the last hint of agony and beckoned forth ecstasy.

I watched like a hawk from behind the seat in front, as more customers took their seats. I was willing to enjoy myself, but not at the expense of discovery. Under no circumstances would I let us be caught – even if it meant ignoring a direct order on Obedience Day.

"Don't pull away," Gary whispered in my ear. "That's an order."

I looked at him in disbelief.

"Unless I order you to."

My head spun and my heart thudded.

"Understand?"

She-sperm twirled around my she-testes.

Another trailer hit the big screen.

"Princess?" he said louder.

"Yes," I snapped, "sir."

He ran his hand faster up and down my she-shaft, placing his thumb over my slit as if to somehow cap my pre-cum.

Yet I could feel myself already leaking.

"Dirty girl."

The sensations from the plug were almost numbing my rear. I needed more. "Next setting," I said quietly.

Gary's eyes widened, then he did as I asked.

I instantly had to slap my palm across my mouth to contain my huskier cries.

A few heads turned.

I bowed my head.

Gary's cock was rock hard in his jeans.

The vibrations from the plug ricocheted into my seat. I was certain people in the rows in front could feel it too.

More were filtering in. It was surely only a matter of if, not when, some decided to take seats in the back row.

The music suddenly stopped. The credits of the final trailer flashed up on screen. The only audible sound in the hushed cinema was the vivid noise of my butt plug.

Yet inside my head there were a million cries of passion and lust.

Someone giggled.

I couldn't stop myself. I was simultaneously humping Gary's hand and gyrating my crack on the plug. Moisture was slipping down my cheeks. I was certain my make-up was running with it.

Gary's palm ransacked my sex.

I bit my hand to contain myself and looked desperately over the back of the seat ahead.

No one was on their feet anymore. Everyone was seated. And we had our row completely to ourselves.

I squeezed Gary's cock through his jeans like I was possessed to destroy it. Yet I wanted only to drain it. Here. Now.

As the British Board of Film Classification threw up on screen their parental guidance for Shrek. In total silence.

Someone crunched on their popcorn.

Someone else sucked soda from their straw.

And then the movie started.

I couldn't take the extremities of pleasure any longer, and tried to cross my legs on Gary's arm.

He manoeuvred his wrist in such a manner he managed to pull my clitty out from my thighs. He relentlessly wanked my sex. "No time outs," he said in my ear.

I looked at him in total disbelief. I was an out and out slave to his strokes. To the vibrations. And powerless to protest in any shape or form.

A shade of green from the screen cast across a devilish glint in his eye. "Obedience Day, slut."

I was nodding before I realised.

"Make out with me. Now."

I threw my mouth to his, caring not in the least if anyone was looking at our row.

Our tongues twisted together.

His hand manipulated my sex in every sense of the word.

My rump rid the plug against my seat for added friction and internal burns.

His lips were sealed tight on my own.

I was panting into his mouth, squashing his mammoth

member with my fingers and ignoring my skirt riding up to my waist. I didn't care. I couldn't care.

Gary's nostrils flared, exhaling over my face.

I hungrily ran my fingers through his hair, wanting a deeper kiss.

The movie, obliviously to us both, played on.

I suppressed a squeal between his lips. Then I had to break our embrace.

He knew from the look in my eyes what was about to happen.

I slammed my ass down hard, then let my clit point up hard and straight in the air.

My lover masturbated her harder and faster, like never before since we'd met. He was furious, funnelling every pound of flesh in his hand back and forth.

My eyes focused first on the film. Then on the blurs of dark heads facing forward below. My body jolted. My head dropped. I watched in awe at myself as my sex spurted cum into the air and onto the back of the seat in front.

Gary forced my legs apart.

I ejaculated more, like the little, wanton whore he must've known I'd always been destined to evolve into.

"Don't stop," he ordered.

I couldn't, lathering the back of the seat in yet more volleys of my she-cream.

Gary's grip on my sex was almost vengeful, determined to drag every last drop out from her.

Until I finished in a panting mess, mesmerised by the experience and almost unaware of my surroundings. I felt sudden cramp in my thighs and a lightness in my head.

Gary let go of my clit, then brought his hand to my mouth.

I understood, and obediently opened my lips.

He fed me my own cum.

I licked my she-sperm from every digit-

A flashlight lit up the entire aisle.

My heart felt like it fell into the depraved depths of my stomach.

Gary whipped his fingers from my face.

I swiftly threw one leg over the other.

The man with the flashlight steadily approached us.

My insides were a mishmash of subsiding excitement and outright fright. How long had he been observing us? How much had he seen?

Gary slipped his hand into his pocket and switched off the plug.

"You two!" the man bellowed. "You need to leave. Now!"

People in front were looking at us, as my humiliation turned my features a whole new colour of crimson.

"What's the problem?" demanded Gary.

"I saw what you were doing to her." He shined the flashlight in my face. "Christ, she's young enough to be your daughter. Get out. Now. Before I call the police."

Gary and I hurried out of the cinema, down the escalators and towards the exit of the mall.

I broke into the best run of my ability, in my stilettos, and started to giggle.

Gary was laughing too.

We couldn't contain ourselves.

And somehow it didn't bother me that people were watching us, wondering what on earth was going on. I felt liberated, despite being thrown out of the cinema. I felt untouchable. Almost invincible.

I reached my hand out.

Gary took it.

We sailed through the exit together.

The afternoon sun blazed down on us.

"I hope you're not too disappointed," he said. "You really wanted to see that film."

I let go of his hand and crossed in front of him to get to the passenger side of my parents' car.

Gary grabbed my arm, spun me around and pinned me against the door.

I gasped-
He planted his lips on mine. In broad daylight.
I opened my mouth.
He shoved his tongue inside.
I was making out with my lover for anyone to see.
He fondled my rear under my skirt.
I felt my mobile vibrate in his pocket against my clitty.
Gary's fingertips pressed hard on my plug, ensuring it sank deeper into my sanctum.

I was literally licking his tongue when he finally broke the embrace. "I need you to fuck me," I whispered.
He grinned.
"I mean it. I *need* it. I'm going out of my mind."
His smile widened.
"You said you would. You told me you'd take me in my parents' bed. You swore to me. You said you'd have orgasm after orgasm inside me there."
Gary pulled my mobile from his jeans.
I watched his facial expression change.
"Shit," he said, then handed me my phone. "You better read that."

MY MOTHER – Your father is getting worse. This is serious. I'm scared xxx

CHAPTER 28

Gary took the car through a tunnel.

My long exhalation gave away my anxiety.

"Has she replied?" he asked.

"No, sir," I said, my reply automated and my mind far from our day of obedience.

He set his hand on my knee. "Try not to worry, baby. I've been sick on holiday before, it always feels worse when you're away from home."

I nodded. "I just have a bad feeling my mother's making it out to be worse than it actually is to be dramatic. You know how she's been, annoyed I haven't been texting her back constantly, asking a hundred and one questions about their trip."

"Well, you know her better than me. She seems more resentful than annoyed, but if she really is doing this just to scare you it's wrong."

"I hope she is," I said.

He squeezed my knee.

I checked my mobile again. There was still no reply.

I shielded my face from prying eyes as Gary reversed the car into our garage.

He shut off the engine, then took my hands in his. "Do you want to call off our little game? I'll understand if your head's not in it after that text."

My eyes widened. "No, sir. I promised you this day, and I'm determined to see it out."

"Are you sure?"

I vehemently nodded. "Give me an order, right now. I'll obey it, without question." My focus took to his crotch.

"There's my girl."

"Anything," I insisted, knowing I'd still to make it all the way from the garage back to the house without being seen. "Your orders terrify me..."

"But, Princess?"

I lifted the front of my skirt to show my she-erection.

He smiled. "My cummy, little mess... Okay, baby... Here's your first order. You're not permitted to shower without my consent or my explicit order. You're to remain as dirty and filthy as you are now, your little clit covered in your dried-up love juice."

"Yes, sir," I said, a little irked but very, very aroused at the idea. "And my second order?"

"You recall the white lingerie we bought yesterday?"

Virgin white!

"I'd like you to retouch your make-up, do something different with your hair and dress up for me in all that sexy, white gear."

"I'd be delighted to, sir. Absolutely! Is there a third order?" Perhaps to get into my parents' bed and await the taking of my virginity?

"Take out your butt plug and clean it, thoroughly. Afford it the wash you must deny yourself."

"Yes, sir. May I be permitted to wear perfume for you?"

Gary thought for several seconds. "Yes." Then he unbuckled his belt, unzipped his fly and pulled his cock out. "Order number four... Give me a handjob."

I walked quickly on my stilettos by the back of the house, my hand, wrist and lower arm drenched in his cum. My heart was pounding as I glanced ahead at the many windows of Jim and Betty's house.

I made it inside, seemingly without incident, and left him behind in the garage, then I quickly set about my duties.

I withdrew my butt plug first, wincing slightly as I expelled it from my anus, then gave it an almost industrious cleaning.

Gary appeared in the kitchen as I was drying it. "Clean?" he asked, shutting the back door behind him.

"Very, sir."

"Let's do a test." He took it from me. "Open wide."

I parted my lips.

Gary shoved it all the way into my mouth, then studied my reaction. "Very good."

I mumbled my reply.

He slipped his hand into his pocket, produced the remote and switched on the vibration.

It was a strange sensation on my tongue.

He upped it to the second setting.

I groaned.

He took it to the third.

I grumbled.

Then the fourth.

I could feel my face a ridiculous series of contortions, but I dared not protest.

He lifted the front of my skirt to check my clitty. "You love being humiliated, don't you, sissy?"

I felt honest when I nodded, despite my blushes.

He switched the vibration off, then took the plug from me. "I'll be in the living room. Let me know when you're ready."

"Yes, sir," I said, and set off to the main bedroom to prepare myself.

"And this kitchen could do with a clean too, sissy. You're not to shirk your housework duties, remember?" he called after me.

"Yes, sir."

MY MOTHER – Your father says you're to stop worrying. I don't agree xxx

ME – I am worried. Very. Please tell me as soon as he starts to get better xx

I set my mobile down on their bed beside me. I *was* genuinely worried, but my mother had cried wolf too many times before. And besides, the sexy feel of the white lace against my chest was just the tonic to take my mind off it. Not to forget the exposed nakedness around my thighs, the sensuous stretch of the suspenders which held up my stockings, the feel of the white nylon on my smoothly-shaved legs and the tightness of the thong encasing my clitty and hauling tightly on my rectum.

The plug inside me had been exciting. It had helped bring me to orgasm. But it'd been nothing less than foreplay for what had to come next.

I breathed casually out as I thought of finally having sex for the first time. Imagining it really happening filled me with thrills rather than frights now. I was ready.

I tied my hair up, revealing my bare neck, and longed for my lover's wonderful kisses. Then I got extra creative, slipping on an expensive silver necklace of my mother's, and went all-out man-eater with my make-up.

Virgin white and a slutty mix of purple mascara and a matching shade of lipstick.

I laid out several condoms across the bed. I was certain he was going to fuck me. There was no other reason for him to choose this outfit. It was perfect for deflowering. But, if I had to, I was going to seduce him.

MY MOTHER – I'm praying he even gets better. You've no idea what I'm going through. How little you understand or care xxx

I felt myself more determined than ever to lose my virginity in her bed.

I'll be in the living room. Let me know when you're ready.

I'd one last text to send, and it wasn't to my mother.

ME – I'm in the main bedroom sir. I eagerly await you. To submit to your superiority and obey your EVERY command xxx

I sat on the edge of the bed, facing the mirror, and waited for him.

There was no immediate movement from the living room, nor reply to my text.

I hadn't expected a reply, and even his delay to come discover his sissy slave was somewhat predictable. This man knew how to frustrate me, to tease me and to have me ready to beg for him to slide his cock inside me.

My sphincter puckered at the prospect.

The living room door opened.

I sat up straight, jutting my chest out as much as I could without the implants I longed for.

Gary paced down the hall, then entered the bedroom.

I saw the implements in his hands in the mirror.

He forcefully placed the leather collar around my neck, locking it in place. "Are you ready to be a good subordinate, cocksucker?"

"Yes, sir."

He hauled the chain, tugging me towards him.

My throat felt instantly sore, like I was being choked. That wasn't a particularly pleasant feeling.

"On the floor, on all fours," he barked.

I did as he demanded, but I tried to look at the bed – to make his eyes follow mine to the condoms I'd put out.

He jerked the leash. "Today isn't about what you want, slut, haven't you realised that?"

"Sorry, sir, I'm stupid and naïve."

He wrapped the chain around his wrist, dragging my throat towards his fist. "You're anything but stupid, sissy."

I panted.

"What? Are you scared?"

I surrendered to a nod. I was whimpering.

"Good... You should be."

I gulped.

Gary strutted forward.

I was dragged after him, and had to motion my palms and knees in quick unison to follow.

He whistled.

I felt I was chasing a losing pursuit, and the pains in my throat were amplified with his every quick step.

Gary led me into the living room, then kicked the door shut behind us.

I could hear my father in my head, giving off angrily about someone slamming it and that *someone had to pay for that.*

He positioned me in the middle of the room, let the leash slacken, then circled me. He took a deep inhalation. "You smell of sex, slut."

I realised I'd forgotten to spray myself with perfume.

"Your own cum. My spunk. You stink of it all."

"Sorry, sir-"

"Like a good whore should."

I smiled.

"Did I order you to smile?"

I quickly lost it.

"You need a lesson in discipline," he said, and removed his belt. "I'm going to ask you some questions. I order you to answer them. I won't order you to tell the truth. I won't even advise it. Let's face it, Princess, it'll be more fun if you're a little liberal with the truth."

I was confused. "Why, sir?"

He swished his belt through the air above my head. "Because I'm going to whip you every time I think you're lying."

What sort of questions? Sexual questions? Or something intellectual I'd know nothing about? "Where are you going to whip me, sir? My ass?"

He slapped the belt across the back of my bare shoulders.

I squealed out, totally unaccustomed to such a violent strike.

"Anywhere I wish, slut."

I took several deep breaths in order to compose myself, then dared look up to him with innocent eyes. "Please don't make me cry, sir, I went to such lengths to please you with my make-up-"

"You look like a whore," he said bluntly.

I looked down. "Yes, sir... *Your* whore."

"Let's begin... Was I the first man you tried to seduce online?"

I hesitated.

He took a step back, ready to hit me with another welt.

"No, sir!"

"*Really?*"

"Yes, sir."

"Explain, quickly."

"I spoke to another man. I was dumb. I gave him my mobile number. He called me. I told him I wanted to suck his cock."

"My dear sissy, I actually think you're telling the truth."

"I am, sir. I was frightened. I masturbated and came quickly, then ended the call."

"How many times did he call you?"

"Just the once, sir-"

Gary smacked my ass hard.

"I'm not lying!" I screamed.

"Why did you not speak to him again, cocksucker?"

"I didn't get his number. He withheld it. I didn't want to speak to him, sir. It was sordid. I felt really dirty. I wasn't ready for that. He wasn't like you."

"Like me, whore?"

"You were so respectful, so caring and reassuring."

"Do you still see me like that?"

I swallowed. Deep down... "Yes, sir."

Gary thrashed the back of my thighs. "Liar!"

"Not right now," I cried. "But I still trust you. I *know* you."

He grabbed my hair in a bunch.

"Please, sir, I tried to make it perfect for you."

His touch turned more tender. "You *did*. I see that. Good girl."

I breathed a sigh of relief that he believed me.

"Was I really your first kiss, sissy?"

"Yes."

He walked around me, surveying me like a predator does his prey. "I genuinely believe you, if only for how you're mollycoddled."

"Thank you, sir."

"It's nothing to be thankful for, Princess. You should've had your fair share of cocks by now."

I was stunned. I thought he really liked me *because* of my

innocence. My virginity.

"Your friend Elaine, she mentioned that her brother came out. Do you know him?"

"No, I-"

Gary cracked his belt against my backside. "The truth, or I'll beat it out of you!"

I steeled my teeth, then struggled to speak through them. "I know who he is. I've seen him around-"

"Do you fancy him?"

"What?" I hadn't even thought about it.

Gary careered his belt right between my buttocks. "Would you suck his cock if he asked you?"

I wheezed.

"Tell the truth, Princess, if I wasn't in your life, and you were dressed right the way you are now, and he was here, stood in front of you with his erect cock in front of your face, telling you to be a good cocksucker, what would you do?"

I stared ahead.

"I *order* you to answer the question," he said.

I visualised Elaine's brother. His bulge. How I remembered it. And. "I..."

The doorbell rang suddenly.

CHAPTER 29

"Oh my God," I whispered. "Aunt Shauna."

Gary quickly refitted his belt.

"Wait, you're not seriously thinking of answering that?"

The doorbell rang again.

"Of course," he said frankly.

WAS HE INSANE!?!

"I'll get rid of her, Princess."

What was he going to do, kick her down the front steps? Knowing this man had a penchant for cruelty, I suddenly couldn't rule it out. "What? How? Don't go out there."

Gary took the handle of the leash and hooked it onto the inside of the living room door. "Just stay here." He opened the door to the hall.

But we had a rule! "No, wait!" If Aunt Shauna was to show up, the game was to be automatically suspended. "Gary!" He agreed to it!

He stopped dead in the doorway. "It's not Gary today... It's sir." He closed the living room door behind him.

I was shaking like a leaf, as I forced myself up from the floor. I was convinced Aunt Shauna was moments away from barging past him. She was certain to find me. Unless I disobeyed him. I quickly lifted the leash from the door.

I heard Gary unlock the front door.

My heart pounded in my chest and perspiration erupted all over my lingerie-clad body. I had to listen. I had to be ready to run and hide in the dining room. Aunt Shauna was most likeliest to storm into the living room, but I couldn't rule out her heading for the kitchen – where the dining room was clearly visible.

"Hello," Gary said loudly, "you're the last person I expected to see."

"Hi, Gary," said a female voice back to him.

Were my ears deceiving me? I felt momentary relief, and placed the leash back on the door handle. I was safe. I could breathe again. *She* would certainly never force her way into my house.

"Why don't you come in, Elaine?" he said.

I was stunned solid.

"Thank you, Gary."

CHAPTER 30

I listened as Gary invited Elaine into the kitchen for coffee. I was still stood in the living room, but the door from the adjoining dining room was open and I could hear every word between them. There was no way for me to make it back to the bedroom via the hall without being seen.

"I'd a funny feeling you'd be here," Elaine said.

"You did?" Gary asked.

"Yeah, there's something I want to say, but I'd rather say it when Mark's here."

"I'm intrigued, Elaine."

Elaine Fucking Bigelow. What the fuck did she want? I nervously toyed with the leash which led between my throat and the living room door handle.

"I'm okay for a coffee, so is he here?" she asked.

"She's around."

"*She?*"

Gary said nothing.

My pulse pummelled my bloodstream.

The door handle turned.

Oh fuck, they hadn't made it to the kitchen yet!

The living room door was pushed open.

Elaine announced, "I really just popped in to see-"

I looked her right in the eye.

"Oh my God." She looked me up and down in my white stockings, suspenders, lace thong, basque, collar and leash. "Mark?"

"Princess," Gary announced proudly behind her.

"Jesus, Mark," she said, turning away, "put some fucking

clothes on!"

I stepped back, horrified.

Gary entered the room. "I told you, Elaine, her name's Princess."

"Gary, pass me a blanket," I said quietly, then dared remove my collar, throwing it behind the door.

Gary retrieved a blanket from beside the sofa.

I threw it around myself, covering all but my stocking-covered calves. But nothing would hide my make-up, nor my fingernails. Or erase the memory of what she'd seen.

Elaine studied me again for a moment, then surrendered a smile. "I knew it. Oh my God, I knew it! I knew it yesterday. You and Mark are together."

I didn't know whether I was more embarrassed at how she was addressing me or how I was dressed.

"I'm so pleased for you both," she continued, entering the room and looking between us. "Mark was so unhappy throughout school. Yesterday was the first I ever saw him look happy."

Gary put his arm around me. "Thank you, Elaine, but we don't call her Mark."

"Princess?" Elaine asked.

I nodded.

"I love it! You two are so sweet!"

"Elaine," I began, my voice wavering between my wish to sound feminine and my nerves absolutely rocking, "you're the only person who knows, and I want to keep it that way."

"Of course!"

"I mean it, my parents can never know."

"I won't tell anyone... Princess."

"No one, Elaine. Not even your brother."

Gary's grip on my shoulder tightened.

"I swear, I won't." Elaine finally looked away from me again. "Speaking of your parents, where are they anyway?"

"They're in Germany for the week," Gary said. "I live at the other end of the country, so it's very difficult for us to see each other."

"I see," Elaine said, and looked at us again, her face seemingly a mixture of surprise and joy. "I'm serious, I knew you two were a couple as soon as I saw you in town. It was so obvious, the chemistry between you is off the charts. You two must've spent all week fucking!"

I almost swallowed my tongue.

Her eyes were all over me again. "So, you like dressing up as a girl?"

I conceded another nod.

"This is amazing. We're similar sizes. We can swap clothes!"

"You're hilarious, Elaine," I said, sarcastically.

"I'm not joking, Princess!" She reached forward and touched Gary's wrist. "I promise you, I'll do everything I can to help her out. Us girlies have to stick together."

"Quite," Gary said. "Princess can't get away from her parents..."

"Uh-huh."

"I was only able to visit this time because they went on holiday."

"Yeah," I said, "and they'll probably never leave me on my own again after the way this week has gone."

"Why, what happened?"

"Oh God, Elaine, one thing after another. My aunt nearly caught us in bed together. Then she saw us together in town yesterday."

Elaine shrugged.

"With two Ann Summers' bags."

"Oh, I see."

"And my dad's taken ill on holiday."

"Oh my God, no. I'm sorry to hear that, Princess." She looked from me to Gary. "Her parents are nice people. They are, don't get me wrong. But I've never met more uptight and over protective people in my life. I mean, I thought mine were controlling until I met hers." Elaine looked to me again, pursing her lips. "They'll never accept *her*."

I breathed a long, anxious exhalation.

"But if I can help you two be together, I'd like to try."

I set my hand in Gary's.

He held it tight.

Elaine smiled again. "You two! You're so right together!"

"Goodbye," Gary said, waving her off, then locked the front door behind her.

I shrugged off my blanket and wrapped myself around him when he re-entered the living room. "I wish you didn't have to go home."

"I know, Princess, me too."

"How do you think that went with Elaine?" I asked.

He rubbed my back through my basque. "To be honest, I got a genuinely good vibe off Elaine from the moment I met her."

I listened.

"I think she could become an important friend to you. It's not good for your mental health to keep your true self locked up all the time."

I guessed I could agree.

"When I go home, Princess, it'll ease my mind knowing you have a friend who knows the real you. One you can talk honestly and openly to..."

"We'll see," I said.

"A confidante..."

Except I still remembered more than Elaine's sweet side in school.

"If not a best friend."

I stroked the side of his face. "I don't want to talk about Elaine Bigelow anymore." I kissed his mouth. "There's really just one thing I want to do for you..."

Gary's eyes drifted to my discarded collar on the floor. "Yes, baby, where were we?"

CHAPTER 31

I ran my bare fingers over the denim outline of Gary's manhood, while dragging his tongue into my mouth. I ran it around with my own, devouring him. I squeezed his crotch, determined to lure him back to bed with me.

His erection throbbed.

I slurped at his saliva.

Gary broke the kiss. "I wish there was a way we could see more of each other, Princess."

"Me too, sir. I want to be your sissy every single day."

"We *must* find a way."

"We will, sir, you're becoming my reason for existing... I have to confess... I'm developing real feelings for you."

"Really?"

I stroked his stubble. "Yes, I know I could make you so happy."

"You already do, slave."

"I want to make you happier, sir." I wanted to replace his wife. "I want to live on a daily diet of your cum." I wanted to move to his part of the country. "I want all my holes stretched out by you everyday." I wanted to move into his house. "I want to be humiliated by you at your every whim."

Gary swiped my panties to one side, exposing my growing clit.

"I want you to laugh at how small she gets."

"Would you show her to a stranger?"

"If you ordered me to, sir. I hope you know that."

He looked into my eyes for several seconds. "I believe you, cocksucker."

"Do you want me to suck your cock now, sir? Or would you rather I gave you something more?"

Gary touched me between my legs. "I can smell your dried cum."

"I've more of yours on my wrist, sir." I leaned in to him for another kiss, but he rebuked me. "I want you so much." I started to unzip his fly. "I've left condoms out on the bed."

"Which bed?"

"My parents' bed, of course."

Gary groaned, as his boxer short-clad bulge broke through his fly.

"My ass yearns for you, sir."

His stomach rumbled.

"Please order me to take you inside me, sir. I long to lose my virginity to you. I'll beg, if that pleases you. Would that please you?"

"Not now, Princess," he said firmly, and drew my hand away from his groin. "Right now, I'm hungry. I want my dinner. You should go attend to your womanly duties in the house, and I'll attend to my manly ones."

I hesitated.

"Sissy?"

I practically stood to attention. "Yes, sir." I started to fix my panties into place.

"What're you doing, you stupid slut?"

I froze.

"Leave your panties to one side. I want your clitty flopping about as you get to work in the kitchen."

"Yes, sir."

As I prepared Gary a dinner of sliced beef, salad and French fries, he entered the kitchen.

"Can I ask an honest question, sir?

"You can ask, whore, but no guarantee you'll get an answer."

I sighed.

"Ask," he commanded, opening a cupboard under the sink.

"Do you really wish I was a slut?"

He lifted out the plastic bag from the bin.

"Sir, do you wish I'd been with other men? A *lot* of other men?"

He kept his back to me.

"Do you wish I wasn't a virgin, is that it?"

He ignored me.

My clitty swished from side-to-side as I stormed across the floor to confront him.

Gary grabbed the handle to the back door.

"Where are you going?" I demanded.

"I'm taking the trash out," he snapped.

"But the neighbours, they could see you. *Again.*"

"I have my manly duties." He pointed to his dinner. "And you have yours. Go take care of them, Princess. Now."

I reluctantly followed his instruction.

"You're lucky I don't attach that leash to the oven."

I spun on my heels to protest-

He slammed the back door shut behind him.

I was getting angrier by the second, fuelled both by the frustration of his continued rejection and his prolonged presence outside. My head was still spinning over Elaine discovering my secret as well. And my heart swung like a pendulum – or my exposed clitty when I walked – between his moods, one moment masked in kindness, the next cloaked in cruelty.

Gary was patrolling the garden, as if deliberately wishing to be seen by the neighbours.

I checked my mobile several times for text messages from my mother, certain Jim or Betty must've made themselves aware of him by now.

"Hello," he shouted, waving.

Except he wasn't waving at me.

I threw my eyes across the wall to Jim and Betty's garden and saw them stood there, watching him.

They both spoke back to him. Neither returned his wave.

"Get in here," I whispered, wishing now more than ever he really could read my mind. "Please, sir. I'll do anything."

I shielded myself from their view behind tilted Venetian blinds and watched the clock as they continued to talk.

Five minutes passed.

What could they be talking about?

Then ten.

When their conversation exceeded fifteen minutes, I was a perspiring mess, mixing with both his and my own dried cum on my body. I was certain I stank worse than a whore.

Twenty minutes.

I was certain he was trying to force my hand, to make me open the back door and call him for his dinner. It was already out of the oven and fully prepared on his plate. I fully expected to be chastised – or worse – if it was cold by the time he ate it.

"Yes, I'll see you again," Gary shouted loudly, and turned to walk down the steps from the garden to the back door.

I stared at him like a furious wraith as he walked in.

"Get that look off your face." He grabbed his plate with one hand. "Follow me to the living room." He flicked my clitty with his other hand.

I winced. "I thought you'd like to eat in the dining room... Off the table."

"I've a better table in mind, slave. And... Bring me a drink."

I strutted into the living room and decided to change tactics, putting more stress on my stilettos, accentuating my hips and swinging my sex further. "There you go, sir," I purred, holding out his drink.

"On the floor," he barked.

I seductively crouched before him and placed the drink by his foot.

"I meant you, slut."

"Sir?"

"Get on the floor, on all fours."

I changed position, as he commanded, and placed my knees and palms on the carpet in the middle of the room.

"Don't be stupid, Princess. Why the hell would I want you all the way over there... Out of reach?"

"Of course, sir, sorry." I shimmied myself quickly to within his touching distance.

"Closer. You need to be so close I can place my knees against you."

I wondered why, but refused to concede to hesitation and moved quickly right in front of him.

"Good girl," he said, then set his plate on my lower back. "There's my table."

His table?!? What? I was to be his makeshift human table? How humiliating! I couldn't imagine anything more demeaning-

"Get your head lower!"

I lowered my head all the way down to the floor, letting my shoulders drop too.

"Good," he said.

I felt the cold rim of his glass suddenly next to his plate.

"I wouldn't want you to spill this beer on your new lingerie."

Or on the carpet! My parents would kill me if beer was spilled anywhere in this house!

Gary took his hand off the glass. "You'd better be very still, Princess."

My clitty throbbed, such was the power of his dominance. "Yes, sir."

"You're going to stay like that until midnight, do you understand?"

Midnight? But at midnight the game would be over. It would no longer be Obedience Day-

He gently spanked my bum. "Answer me, whore."

"Yes, sir," I said quickly and firmly, fearful of spillage, and maintained a straight spine.

"I do hope you understand the consequences..."

I did. All too well.

Gary switched on the television.

I wasn't even facing it.

He laughed out loud.

I didn't know if he was laughing at something he could see on screen, or the pathetic virgin before him.

He stuck his fork into a slice of roast beef, then cut it with his knife.

I struggled hard to maintain my composure.

Gary caught his glass. "You stupid cocksucker, you almost spilled that already!"

"Sorry, sir," I said quickly, my mind trying to ascertain why he seemed intent on refusing to fuck me.

"You have to last like this until midnight. You will not be moving from this position, no matter what. I hope I've made myself clear on that matter?"

"Yes, sir."

"These are your final orders, Princess... You'll be receiving no more from me."

CHAPTER 32

It felt like several hours had passed, and I'd barely moved. Like, not even as much as an inch. I'd not spoken to Gary, and responded only with movement when he sternly warned me I was slacking and that some beer was spilling over the edge of the glass. I'd barely felt it, but the thought of ruining my new lace basque – or, worse still, wrecking the carpet – spurned me on to correct my posture.

He hadn't touched his beer. It was there purely for this exercise. All he'd done was watch television and ignore me.

I couldn't understand of all the sexual things he could've ordered me to do, this is what he made his final order. And I couldn't even stick my thong-clad ass out in front of the television to try to tempt him into touching me. Not unless I wanted to be covered in beer. And to covet his disappointment.

"You're doing very good, baby," Gary said finally. "Not long to go now."

I pathetically felt glee at his praise.

He laughed aloud.

I hoped it was at something on the television and not my stupidity.

He drummed his fingers.

It was only after several seconds I realised he was drumming on my lower back. I'd become numb, and quickly corrected my shape.

"That was a close one," he quipped. "The beer was almost all over you."

I suppressed my emotions.

"I know you want to complain, sissy. It's written all over

you... And not just in beer and cum."

I ignored his contemptuous laughter, and wondered if perhaps I was coming to predict his behaviour more so than he realised. After all, as soon as he'd had me get on all fours and informed me of my orders I was certain he'd ignore me for a long time. As I expected, he was becoming more rattled than me. I knew his next attempt to spill some beer would be more severe. I'd need to be ready.

But maybe he was becoming even more predictable than that. I surmised there was a chance, perhaps even an inevitability, that if I successfully kept the beer still on my back until midnight he'd drag my ass to bed and take my virginity. He wouldn't have to order me. It'd be mutually consensual. It would be my reward.

Unless... What if he just decided to fuck me right here, right now? He could use the new dildo on me, to preserve my virginity. How could I possibly keep the beer still then? I'd have a heart attack if it spilt – and he knew it.

"Well done, Princess!" he yelled aloud.

I remained frozen in place.

"You did it."

My eyes were still focused on the floor. "I did?"

"It's midnight."

"It is?" I asked, almost in disbelief.

He leapt forward, knocking his hand into the glass. "Oh shit!"

I felt it fall backwards on me.

"Sorry!"

A pint of stale, warm beer flushed down my lower back and cold buttocks. "The floor!" I cried out, and started to scramble forward, ready to set about cleaning it.

Gary grabbed my throat in one hand and my side, just above my hips, with the other. He stilled me easily. "Wait, sissy, you didn't make it. I was on the wrong television channel. It's midnight in France. It's only eleven here."

"The carpet, sir, I need to clean the carpet or my parents will kill me!"

"I'll kill you... If you dare move."

I gulped.

He waited in silence, holding me still.

I resisted for several seconds, trying to free myself, until finally I conceded to his superior strength.

"Let me remind you of your orders, sissy. You must not move, therefore you must leave the beer where it is and remain in that position. It's a true test of your obedience."

I could smell it staining the carpet with my every inhalation. "But I've nothing to balance, sir." And an hour to go.

Gary threw his legs onto my back. "You do now, slut."

CHAPTER 33

I was exhausted as Gary dragged my aching body, by the leash, up the hall. I was still unwashed, my rear saturated in beer and my wrist and groin smelling of cum. I yearned to be clean, as the bathroom door came into view. It was after midnight, after all. I could do what I wanted again, without having to ask. But I was beat. And I'd been beaten.

I allowed myself to be hauled past the bathroom and into my parents' bedroom.

Gary swept the condoms off the bed and onto the floor on my mother's side. He drew back the duvet. "Get in, baby," he said.

"Yes, Gary," I replied, then detached the collar from around my throat and let it fall to my father's side with the leash.

Gary eyed me as if I'd defied him.

I had. "The game's over."

He watched me crawl into my father's side and lie on my front.

I was so tired I knew I'd provide him nothing but a lifeless, rotten whore of a carcass to fuck – if he even wanted to at all.

Gary removed his clothes.

I strained to keep one eye open on him. I felt a sense of shame underneath disappointment when I saw his cock was soft.

He went to the bathroom.

I listened to him urinate loudly, then use the makeshift shower in the bath and finally brush his teeth. I didn't even have the energy to tuck my sex back between the front of my panties.

He tucked the duvet around my body when he returned, then slipped into my mother's side beside me. "You were incredible today, Princess," he said after a minute, as he stroked my cheek.

"Would you like me to let your hair down?"

I nodded.

He gently removed the clips I'd used to hold it in place.

"Were you *really* happy with my performance over the last twenty-four hours, Gary?"

He nodded.

I felt confusion overwhelm any sense of satisfaction.

"It didn't seem like a performance, Princess. It seemed like you were exploring a side of yourself. Tell me, were you acting when you enjoyed being humiliated?"

I neglected to answer.

"On reflection, I don't think you were. And I certainly didn't in the moment." He slipped his arm around me and cuddled up.

Who are you? I was looking at him, but I was also asking myself.

He yawned.

I felt no sign of an erection, semi or otherwise, against me.

"Goodnight, Princess," he said, and kissed as close to my lips as he could manage.

"Goodnight..." I couldn't say lover, not when he hadn't... "Gary..."

"Yes, baby?"

I stared into his eyes. "Why?"

"Why what?"

I knew he knew what I meant.

"Elaborate," he said.

I felt myself instinctually drawn to obey and answered immediately, "Why didn't you order me to let you fuck me?"

"Because you're not ready for it."

I felt my heart break as he closed his eyes.

He looked at total ease.

Despite all my loss of energy and 24 hour denial of free will, I mustered the might to demand, "What?"

"Sissy, I'd never make you do anything you're not ready for."

I couldn't believe what I was hearing. How dare he! It was my body. "I *am* ready, lover."

He said nothing.

I somehow threw my palm to his chest, as if pleading with his heart to hear me. "I know I am."

He ignored me.

"Won't you even discuss it with me?"

He didn't flinch.

I felt his heart beat gently against my palm. My own thundered upon the mattress. I withdrew my hand from him, then fought not to choke on the lump in my throat, nor to surrender to the tears ready to stream from my eyes.

Gary casually exhaled.

"Of all the things you said and did to me today," I whispered, not only had that hurt more than anything but, "I am further away from understanding you than ever."

His face remained the same as he spoke, "And you wonder why I say you're not ready."

CHAPTER 34

I slept late on Thursday morning, no doubt due to the emotional and physical endurance of Obedience Day. I rolled onto my back, then stretched to switch on my father's bedside radio. The sound of Gorillaz's Clint Eastwood rang out.

Gary was not beside me. I wasn't sure where he was.

I forced myself to sit up and stretch, coming face-to-face with my reflection in the mirror of the wardrobe. I'd slept in my make-up. Face down. I wasn't pretty. And I stank.

The lyrics of the song shook themselves around my head.

I watched myself. I watched the vacancy in the bed beside me. I heard the last things Gary had said to me the night before. I peeled the duvet away from my body and looked at myself in my sexy, white lingerie – albeit splashed in beer. I had the perfect figure. My hair was a dishevelled mess. And although my make-up was distorted by the night, I felt a strange confidence about myself. He would be lucky to have me. Obedience or not.

I felt a determination rising up inside.

I wouldn't need to change, nor shower, nor retouch my make-up.

I was going to prove to Gary I was ready for sex. Not tonight. Not this afternoon. Now.

I was going to seduce him.

I was going to show him.

He was going to succumb to his natural urges. He was going to be consumed, compelled and overwhelmed.

I strutted with purpose down the hall, letting my hips sway sexily with the enhanced height of my stilettos, and, with only a dash of perfume to dispel my stench, I knew I looked skanky. Slutty. And, in no way through illusion, in serious need of the fucking of my life.

I ignored the wide open curtains and threw caution to the wind as I set my painted fingertips on the door handle to the living room, and quickly opened it.

Gary was sat on one sofa, sipping coffee. He looked surprised to see me.

Then, as I opened the door further, I saw Elaine holding a cup and sat on the other.

"Oh God, Mark- I mean, Princess," she said, and swiftly looked down. "You didn't know I was here."

"No," I said, my heart still thudding with adrenaline. "Gary, can I-"

"No need to change, baby," he commanded, and beckoned me next to him. "Join us."

I was certain I failed to disguise my irritation, as I automatically obeyed him and curled up next to him, sitting my thong-clad ass on my calves and setting my hands in one of his.

Elaine watched us. "You two are so in love," she cooed.

I feared how deep my feelings were.

Gary squeezed my hands.

I knew he didn't truly feel the same way.

"How is this going to continue when your parents get back?"

I looked at her and shrugged.

"That's not good enough. Gary, speak to her. Tell her to see sense."

"Princess has a lot of growing up to do, Elaine."

I felt my little clitty shrivel inside my panties.

"True, but are you really going to go home and break her heart?" Elaine uncrossed her denim-clad legs and sat forward, setting her coffee at her crotch. "It's not right."

"It's where my life is," he said.

I felt my heart pang at his bluntness.

"And you're not going to fight for him... Are you, Princess?"

My head was swimming. I didn't know what to say.

"Well?" she demanded.

"I don't know, Elaine," I said so timidly I couldn't look at her.

She pointed at me. "I've been thinking about all this. In fact, it's all I thought about yesterday when I went home. I spoke to my brother-"

"Elaine! You said you wouldn't tell anyone!"

"Keep your panties on, I didn't name names. I just had to speak to someone else for perspective..."

I knew her. She'd outed me. And Gary would interrogate me on what that'd mean for us if Elaine's brother got in touch with me after he left.

"He was sympathetic. He gets this. And we both see this the same..."

Gary gently, reassuringly stroked his thumb over my hands.

"It's difficult for you to meet. The logistics aren't good. And your parents are so overbearing they wouldn't let you travel alone. And you'd fucking let them." Elaine pointed at Gary. "You're married, aren't you?"

"Yes," he said finally.

"So even if she does get away to meet you at yours it's not practical... That's where I come in."

"Enlighten us."

I shivered at his touch on my hands and the warmth of groin beneath. I needed this man so much. I was crazy. I was supposed to be seducing him right now!

"Next summer," she began, "I want to travel. I want to go to Amsterdam. Princess could come with me..."

Amsterdam? I just knew the first thing my parents would think of when they heard Amsterdam was drugs. And the second thing would be prostitutes.

"You could meet us there, Gary."

I'd have to wait a whole fucking year to see him again?!?

"We'd have a year to work on her parents, we'd get their blessing..."

The room turned strangely silent. Was he that dead set against the idea of seeing me again?

"And then Mr Handsome over there can spend day after day pumping that sweet, tight ass of yours, Princess."

I was gobsmacked, and my face surely told.

"Oh, come on," she said, "you really think there's any doubt who the bottom is here?"

I glared at her. I knew she'd told her brother everything about me. Those words had come straight from his mouth. And secrets around here didn't stay secrets for very long. I'd be the talk of the town in no time. And my parents would find out. I'd be kicked out-

"I love it," Gary said. "Amsterdam it is, baby."

I swivelled my head to face him. "Really? You'd fly out to meet me... Well, us." I didn't want to even look at her right now.

"One hundred percent." He leaned forward to look at Elaine. "She does have a sweet, tight ass, doesn't she?"

"She does... Lucky bitch."

I felt the fire in his loins through my fingers. I couldn't help myself. I kissed his lips right in front of my former classmate. "Thank you, Gary. Thank you so much. Oh God, you don't know how much this means to me, knowing I'll get to see you again."

He gestured to Elaine with a nod. "Thank your friend there."

My... Friend? I turned to her.

She was smiling widely.

"Thank you... Elaine."

"Don't mention it, Princess. You and me are going to be the best of girly friends. I'll be your confidante for all things Gary when he goes... You can trust me, Gary."

"I know, Elaine. I can see that."

I was caught in the middle of what felt like some kind of conspiracy, yet I felt comforted – blessed, even – by the idea.

"I'll do anything I can to help you two meet up in the future," Elaine said. "Hey, maybe my parents will go away and you two can stay at mine."

I dared look at her and wondered, *what was this going to cost me?*

She looked at the clock, then swiftly set her cup on the floor.

"Oh shit, the time. I better go." She threw herself to her feet, then looked at the spot on the carpet where I'd balanced beer the night before. She pointed as she giggled. "I can only imagine what those stains are."

I gulped.

"I'll see myself out." She hurried across the floor to the door. "You two probably wanna get right back at it."

"Bye, Elaine, thanks again for everything."

"Anytime, Gary."

Gary squeezed my hands.

"Thanks, Elaine."

We listened to her shut the front door behind herself.

"You're gonna owe her big time for that, baby. She's really doing us a favour."

"I know," I whispered. I brushed the thought temporarily aside, pulled my hands from within his palm and leaned in for another kiss, hoping this time it'd be deeper, longer and lead finally to sex between us.

CHAPTER 35

Gary turned his mouth away.

I couldn't take another rejection, and clawed at his stubble, striving to pull his lips to mine.

"No, Princess," he barked.

"Kiss me, Gary. Please. Take me here now. Fuck me."

"No."

My clitty slipped out from within my panties as I tried to straddle him. "It's already Thursday. We're running out of time."

He seized hold of my wrists, then held me at bay.

I was burning with desire for him. I started to grind my sex against his crotch. "I need you inside me, lover. I need it so much."

"Look at you," he said. "You look like a whore. You smell like a whore."

"I wanna be *your* whore," I rasped, and dragged my legs to either side of his stomach so I could rub my rear on his rising erection. "I can feel you. I know you want me too."

"I don't want a whore today. I want you at your ladylike best. Go get cleaned up. All I can smell is spunk and stale booze."

I froze.

"I need *my* Princess back today." He gently released his hold on my wrists. "That perfect girl I adore."

I reluctantly surrendered my sexual resolve.

"You'll go get cleaned up, baby?"

I nodded. "I'll comply." I'd do anything to have him.

His cock was so warm and hard beneath me. "But you don't just need a shower, Princess." He gestured to the room around him. "This house needs tidied too."

"And then you'll play with me?"

He stroked my face. "Then, Princess, my darling, virgin sissy... I'll do more than play with you."

"More?" I demanded.

"I'll penetrate you."

I was giddy as I stripped off my dirty lingerie and dumped the items in the wash basket. I tested the water in the shower. It was warm enough for a good clean.

My mobile beeped in the bedroom.

MY MOTHER – Your father is severely ill. I'm at my wit's end. I've been talking on the phone with your Aunt Shauna. What the hell is up with her? There's something seriously wrong with her mental state. It's like she thinks that Gary guy is trying to get you into a cult. I know I can be overprotective of you, but I know my son and you're much smarter than that. I put Shauna in her place. How are you? XXX

My mother had just said the word hell. It was like someone else entirely had written her text. Yet, still I knew my mother.

ME – I'm ok! I'm fine! I'm not in a cult or anything at all! I don't know what's wrong with her. Tell dad I love him xx

Except I knew exactly what was wrong with Aunt Shauna. She knew what Gary and I were doing together. I could feel it in my veins.

I stepped naked into the shower.

I dried myself after a thorough clean, having rinsed off every shred of evidence I'd ever been a slave to cum and balancing beer. The red marks from Gary's belt on my back, bum and legs would have to heal themselves, however.

I smiled at the thought of still having them after he left.

I frowned at the thought of him leaving.

I want you at your ladylike best.

I checked my fingernails. They were beginning to chip.

I headed to the bedroom and used my mother's nail polish remover, figuring a fresh start with a new colour might impress Gary.

I'd just taken off the last remnant of my previous colour when I realised Gary was calling me. I went to the door to the hall.

"Yes?" I called back.

"Come here," he shouted.

"I'm not ready." I hadn't even decided what I was going to wear for him. "Give me another twenty minutes." I *really* wasn't in the mood to clean the house, even though the thought of those beer stains on the carpet was irking me more with every minute.

"I don't care. Come in here."

I sighed. "Gary, I'm not even dressed yet!"

He released a familiar, devilish guffaw. "Even better... The dining room... *Now*."

I ignored the undrawn curtain, again, as I walked naked into the kitchen and towards the dining room. "Gary, what's this a-"

On the dining room table, sheathed in a condom and stood upright, was the new dildo we'd got in Ann Summers.

"'Bout?" I finished, stuttering to a shimmering halt.

All ten magnificent inches of the dildo glistened with whatever he'd found to use as a lube. The bulging veins threatened with lifelike authenticity. The bulbous head was a sheer monster, ready to tear a vagina – never mind a virgin ass – apart.

Gary stood beside it in just a pair of tight, white underpants, his cock already visibly semi-rigid underneath. "You need to know what it's like to fuck something like this-"

I grabbed his arm. "No, Gary, I need the real thing." I tried to make for his rod-

He swatted my hand away.

"I need yours."

"You're not ready," he said firmly. "And you will do as you're told."

I huffed.

"You're going to climb up on this table and sit on this dildo."

I puffed.

"You're going to ride it through whatever agony it brings you..."

I panted.

"And you're going to cum while doing it..."

I gasped.

"Or you won't lose your virginity to me before I leave-"

"Before you *go home*," I snapped, with such immature cheek I cowered almost immediately.

He wagged his finger at me. "Don't give me more cause to think you're unready for full sex, Princess." He slid his underpants down to the floor.

My eyes flicked between the gargantuan cock on the table and the real thing before me. I was in awe of both. Both *were* impressive. But there was no escaping the size difference. The dildo dwarfed even Gary's mammoth member. "I'm not even wearing any make-up yet."

"Nonsense." Gary pulled out a chair and began to help me up on it to get onto the table.

"Is this a test?" I asked.

"Of course."

"No, Gary, I mean is this a trick question type of thing?"

He looked puzzled.

"Am I being forced to choose between the dildo and your cock? Like if I sit on the dildo, are you going to punish me by denying me your cock again?"

He shook his head.

"Please, Gary, I *need* your cock inside me so much. I want it so bad. You've no idea. All I can think about it is taking it in my ass pussy."

He manoeuvred me until I was squatting over the head of the dildo.

"Please, don't trick me, Gary." I was so wanton, I felt maniacal in my desires. "I think I'll die if I don't get to make love to you."

He started to push down on my shoulders.

I could feel the brute of the head at my entrance.

"There's a good girl," he whispered.

"Gary, please don't make me do this."

He moved his hands to under my arms. "Release all your bodyweight to me."

I slowly surrendered until all of me was being held in his hands. I was using no muscles in my legs to hold myself above the dildo. "It's too big, Gary, please have mercy on me."

He gave me a reassuring smile, as he lifted me an inch or so off the table. "Princess, on a scale of one to ten, how much do you need to experience a cock inside you?"

"Ten!" I screamed.

Gary dropped me.

CHAPTER 36

Intolerable, agonising pain overwrought my entire body as my rectum was ripped open around the almighty circumference of the dildo.

Gary surged forward, catching my cries in one palm and hauling me upwards with his other.

"Hello? Mark? Gary? Anyone here?"

Shock suppressed the last of my squeals.

Gary lifted me off the table and set me down naked on both feet.

"Where are you?" she slurred.

Neither of us had remembered to lock the front door after Elaine left!

Gary grabbed his white underpants from the floor and helped me into them.

I stumbled, my mind in a daze and my body at war with reality.

"It's your aunt," he whispered. "She's here. She can't see us together like this." He side-stepped from the doorway to the kitchen to behind the adjoining wall of the dining room.

I was frozen, trapped within male underwear again.

Gary swiped the dildo from the table. "Go. Get rid of her."

"Mark, where're you hiding?"

Gary trailed me by my elbow, then shoved me into the kitchen.

My innards were still wide open, and pulsating too.

"Oh," she said, stopping suddenly in the doorway between the hall and the kitchen. Her eyes were locked on me in my state of undress.

"Aunt Shauna," I mustered.

"A cult," she whispered.

"I wasn't expecting you."

"Gary!"

"Aunt Shauna, please..." I stepped toward her.

"Where is he, Mark? I know he's here!"

I tried to ignore the fact my clitty felt so ridiculously tiny in his oversized, baggy briefs.

"Gary!" she cried out, and whirled around. "I'll find you!"

I chased after Aunt Shauna, as she stormed into the spare bedroom.

"Not here."

I was pushed aside as she marched up the hall.

"Gary!"

My insides curled as I thought of all the condoms he'd swept onto the floor on my mother's side of the bed.

Aunt Shauna poked her head into my parents' bedroom.

I held my breath.

She silently stepped inside.

Oh fuck. I was done if she found them.

Aunt Shauna looked at the bed.

I'd made a half-hearted attempt to make it earlier, but compared to my mother's meticulous methods it was plain to see it'd been slept in.

She spun around. "Gary!"

At least to me.

She barged past me and entered my own bedroom.

I followed her. "Aunt Shauna, what's going on?"

"I know that man's here, Mark. I know what he's doing to you."

"Have you been drinking?" I asked.

Aunt Shauna sent a back-handed slap towards me.

I snapped out of the way, avoiding it, but stumbled back and hit my ass against the door. I winced and let out a sissified cry as my anus contracted upon impact. "Please, stop this. Aunt Shauna, I'm begging you. No one's here-"

"Gary!" she screamed, giving the bedroom one final survey, then headed out to the hall again.

I chased desperately behind her.

She entered the kitchen. "Come out here and face me like a man!"

How the fuck was I going to convince her he wasn't here?

"Tell me what you've been doing to my nephew!"

Neice.

"I know you're-"

I watched as she stopped speaking suddenly, then stomped her feet through the kitchen towards the dining room. My heart almost stopped.

She walked in. She stopped. She looked to her right.

I froze.

"Gary," she said.

I felt something leak from my rear.

Aunt Shauna pounded her feet into the living room.

I stepped timidly into the dining room. There was no sign of Gary or the dildo. The living room was clear too.

Aunt Shauna staggered in a semi-circle. "I *know* that man's here, Mark."

"He's not here, Aunt Shauna."

"I can smell him," she declared.

I smelt only stale booze, and I wasn't sure if it was coming from her or the carpet.

She started to walk around the room. She looked behind one sofa. Then another.

I breathed again when she found nothing. "That's every room you've checked."

She looked at me, her eyes running up and down my body. "No, you stupid boy, not every room."

I watched in horror as she left the living room like a one woman stampede. Gary had to be hiding somewhere. I was certain he wouldn't be hard to find. And he was fucking naked.

She charged into the bathroom.

I quickly followed.

The curtain was pulled across the bath.

My aunt looked at me. "I should've dragged you out of here the first time I found him with you." She reached her hand out to the curtain.

"Aunt-"

She ripped it back.

Gary wasn't there.

"What's this about?" I asked, sounding even more stupid than I felt.

"Get dressed," she snapped. "You're coming with me."

I dressed quickly in my bedroom, my aunt stood over me, watching my every move and keeping her ears at the ready for the slightest sound from anywhere else in the house.

"Where are we going?" I asked.

"Anywhere, as long as you're away from that man."

"He isn't here, Aunt Shauna. I don't know what this is about-"

"Really?" Her eyes were on my legs.

I pulled up my jeans in a rush. "How'd you get here?"

"I got the bus."

I *hated* the bus, but maybe it was best I left the car behind for Gary. Then I could text him to come pick me up after I'd calmed Aunt Shauna down in an hour or so.

She swiped my mobile up before I could slip it into my pocket. "I'll be confiscating this," she said, and dropped it into her purse. "Now, go get your mother's keys. You're driving, Mark. And we're out of here."

I silenced a sigh.

"Unless..."

"Unless what, Aunt Shauna?"

"Unless Gary feels like revealing himself now and giving me the proper respect and explanation a loving aunt deserves..."

We waited in silence for several seconds.

A part of me wished he'd appear, miraculously fully dressed and charming as ever, to win her over and get rid of her for good – and without humiliating me. But I knew that was impossible.

"That's what I thought," she said. "Let's go."

CHAPTER 37

"But *where* are we going, Aunt Shauna?" I asked, perplexed to the direction of the country road leading us ever further from the city... And Gary.

"Never mind, buttercup, just drive."

I'd asked her to stop calling me that when I was 10 years old. Tens years later and still she persisted.

"We're going to get to the bottom of what's going on between you and Gary."

I changed into a lower gear and rounded a particularly tight bend between hedge-lined fields. "There's nothing *going on*, Aunt Shauna, I haven't the faintest idea what you're talking about."

"Ha!"

I sighed. "Can I have my mobile back please?"

"No." She turned it over in her hand. "I'm convinced Gary will try to make contact with you."

I too was terrified he would.

"And I intend to answer it and hear what he has to say."

I was pretty sure he'd know better than to speak first.

"Or read what he texts you."

Shit.

"Take a left up ahead," Aunt Shauna barked.

"But my mother might text," I protested. "My father's not well. He's ill-"

"She'll phone *me*, Mark. I'm her sister."

I watched my Aunt's hand as she turned the low volume on the radio even lower. Her hand was shaking.

"Stop there!"

I almost slammed the brakes in a panic, and only just

remembered to check my mirrors before I brought the car to a halt outside a cottage. "Here, Aunt Shauna?"

"Yes, Mark." She pointed to the property. "There's Madam Scarah, waiting for us."

I looked into the driveway and saw a distinctive woman, easily in her late 50s, dressed in a long, flowing black dress with a multicoloured, unbuttoned cardigan over her shoulders. She had long white hair and a crooked nose, like a witch.

She beckoned us with one finger.

Aunt Shauna unfastened my seat belt. "You go first, Mark. And give me the keys. You're *not* getting out of this."

The witch-like woman led us down the hall of the cottage, through the kitchen and finally into the dining room.

"Sit," she said, gesturing to four empty seats around a circular table.

Aunt Shauna nodded at me to take the seat at the head of the table, the furthest from the front door. Then she sat to my left.

The witch sat opposite me.

The seat to my right remained empty.

There were several scented candles around the room, and one alight in the centre of the table. A deck of cards were overturned to one side of the candle. And a white bowl, filled with what I assumed was water, was placed at the other.

The witch looked up to the ceiling, closed her eyes and muttered something quietly and incoherently to herself.

"Who's this again?" I whispered to my aunt.

She shushed me.

"Is she supposed to be a psychic?"

Aunt Shauna kicked me under the table.

I couldn't think of any dead people I even knew.

The witch lowered her neck, then opened her eyes on mine. She had a unique ability to somehow look at me, through me and into me all at the same time.

I felt a little unnerved.

"Introduce yourselves," the witch said.

I figured she wasn't much of a clairvoyant if she needed us to tell her our names.

"I'm Shauna, Madam Scarah, as you know... And this is my nephew-"

"Let... *Him*... Speak for themselves."

Aunt Shauna's reaction was even more puzzling than my own.

"Mark," I said reluctantly.

Madam Scarah arched one eyebrow. "Are you sure?"

I was pretty sure this was neither the time nor the place to announce myself as Princess. "Yes."

Madam Scarah dipped both her sets of fingertips into the water, then flicked the water at me.

I reeled momentarily backwards, hitting the back of my chair noisily off the glass patio doors behind me. "Sorry," I said, a little breathlessly. "I wasn't expecting that." I made a nervous laugh.

Aunt Shauna tutted.

Madam Scarah touched the top card on her table. "Why are we here today?"

"I told you," Aunt Shauna said. "On the phone. Last night."

Oh God, this was off to a great start. A medium, witch or whatever she was who couldn't even remember why we were here.

"Didn't I?" Aunt Shauna asked.

Madam Scarah bolted upright. "I see a man..."

Puh-lease.

"With the letter G."

"Gary," Aunt Shauna snapped. "I knew it."

"Aunt Shauna, you just said you spoke to Madam Scarah last night. You told her to say that, didn't you?"

"Madam Scarah, I believe Gary has somehow got an evil spirit to possess Mark. Look at him, *really* look at him, that's not how he normally looks."

No, normally I dressed up in sexy lingerie, wore make-up and shoved my lover's dick in my mouth. But, unfortunately, today I was stuck in a pair of his briefs. Although the feel of

Gary's underwear against my skin was both excruciating and delightful. I hated being robbed of my time with him, and the feel of his underwear was my only comfort.

"There's an evil spirit inside him," Aunt Shauna said, accidentally spitting saliva as she spoke.

Madam Scarah searched me with her eyes.

"I'd say the only spirits in the room are coming off your breath, Aunt Shauna."

My aunt shot me a look that could kill.

I looked down, scorned.

"You're uncomfortable in the cloak you wear," Madam Scarah said.

Cloak?

"You know what I mean, don't you?"

Did she mean Gary's underwear? "It's okay," I muttered. "I guess."

"Your face is not your own."

Aunt Shauna pressed her forefinger on the table. "I knew it, Madam Scarah. Mark's possessed, isn't he?"

My mobile beeped in Aunt Shauna's purse.

"No," Madam Scarah said, dipping the fingers of her free hand in the bowl of water again.

I braced myself for another shower.

"I use the term face in a metaphorical sense, Shauna. This *is* Mark, but it's as if Mark is not Mark's true self how he appears before us."

Shit.

Madam Scarah didn't blink as she stared at me.

Was it possible she could truly see the real me?

"I see you," she said.

Fuck.

"Yes, there you are... And you know I see you."

I tried to silently beg for her discretion with my eyes.

Aunt Shauna grabbed Madam Scarah's wrist. "You need to perform an exorcism. Right now. Don't delay or the demon will take deeper control."

Madam Scarah eyeballed Aunt Shauna's fingers wrapped around her wrist. "That..."

Aunt Shauna removed her hand.

"Would..."

I gulped.

"Be..." Madam Scarah rested her eyes on me again. "Premature."

"Premature?" Aunt Shauna demanded. "Delaying it'd be a disaster!"

"Untimely, at best, I assure you," Madam Scarah said.

Aunt Shauna banged her fist on the table. "This is ridiculous, he's possessed!"

"Join hands with me," Madam Scarah said, reaching hers across the table towards mine.

I didn't want to.

"Don't be afraid, I won't hurt you... P."

I almost half-grinned.

"Come, my dear, trust me."

Somehow, I found myself lending my palms to Madam Scarah's. I was immediately struck at how smooth her skin felt, despite her years. I didn't feel as frightened as before.

She locked her eyes on mine, yet it was a soft lock.

I felt obliged to stare back.

Madam Scarah smiled to me.

"What on earth are you doing?" Aunt Shauna rasped.

It was as natural as night turning to day when I started to smile back.

Madam Scarah rubbed her thumbs on my hands. "I see you, child. I see the real you. I see what has been happening... And I see soon you will be a child no more."

My virginity would be taken?

"What?" Aunt Shauna yelled, totally irate.

"I will light a candle for you tonight, and it will burn through until tomorrow evening. I think you'll understand by then."

I... Did?

Madam Scarah gave me a final, broader smile, then released

my hands. "There is no possession here."

"What? Madam Scarah, you said P. You must've meant possessed. Do an exorcism *now*, I insist."

"Shauna, I shall do no such thing-"

"But I'm paying you. Get this demon out of my nephew, I order you!"

Madam Scarah shook her head. "That won't be necessary. This beautiful person before me is not possessed, not in the slightest, but there is trouble when it comes to identity and acceptance."

Aunt Shauna looked between us.

"But you'll be fine, child. You will find yourself."

"Thank you," I said quietly, my cheeks a little rosy.

"But, Madam Scarah, you mentioned Gary. You said G. Is he a danger to Mark?"

"Mark?" Madam Scarah asked.

Aunt Shauna pointed her finger so close to me she almost jabbed my eye. "Him! My nephew!"

Madam Scarah shook her head. "Gary's a guardian... But not to the Mark I see."

Aunt Shauna slid her chair backwards into the wall and stood. "This is utter claptrap. I want a refund!"

"No refunds," Madam Scarah said, then gestured to the kitchen. "You may leave the same way you entered."

Aunt Shauna huffed and puffed. "Come along, Mark. We're leaving!"

Aunt Shauna did up her seatbelt, then tossed me the keys. "Drive."

"Where?" I asked.

"Anywhere, I don't care."

I started the engine, as Aunt Shauna dug into her purse and produced my mobile.

"I might've known," she said, turning the screen of my phone towards me. "And don't tell me *he's* psychic."

GARY – Where did you go?

"He was in that house, Mark... That proves it."

I took a deep breath, then asked, "Can't I just go home, Aunt Shauna?"

"That's the last place you'll be going today... *Child*." She slipped my mobile back into her purse. "Now, drive."

After nearly an hour, the country roads swept aside and gave way to the suburbs. I took note of a golf course to one side of the road as Aunt Shauna spotted a newsagent's.

"Stop there," she said.

I did as I was told without a word.

"Keys."

I handed them over.

Aunt Shauna sauntered off into the shop, purse in hand.

I waited, impatiently, for her to return.

Five minutes later, she appeared looking a little flustered and got into the car. She held up a paper sleeve with an unseen magazine inside. "There's something here I want you to look at, Mark."

"Okay," I said.

My aunt turned the sleeve upside down, and out slipped an adult pornographic magazine.

I saw the blonde hair and the big boobs for a split-second, then instinctively looked away.

She grabbed my wrist. "Look at it, Mark. You have to!"

"No, Aunt Shauna, you're embarrassing me."

"Come off it, Mark. Gary made out you're addicted to this sort of stuff. So, go ahead. Take a look. I won't judge."

I reluctantly let her thrust the mag into my hands.

"Open it," she insisted.

I forced myself to overcome my hesitance, and opened the first page. It was merely a contents page, so I skipped forward. Suddenly, I was looking at a girl with an admittedly amazing figure, tight waist, pert breasts and – what I'd never have – a little, shaven pussy. I was sure men would fall instantly for her. I flicked on. The next few pages were of similar nudes. I didn't know whether to feign interest, as perspiration overwhelmed my body, or to give in to my obvious shame. I was sat next to my aunt, for goodness' sake. No part of this was right. And then I found a girl with a bum just like mine, clad in stockings and-

Aunt Shauna snatched the magazine from me and stuffed it back in the sleeve. "Another lie, Mark. You're not a bit interested in porn, are you?"

I sighed, unable to answer.

"Your mother and I might not approve of these types of magazines, but we're not stupid. We know what men are like."

Why couldn't she just leave me alone?

"I swear, Mark, I'll get to the bottom of what's been going on before your mother gets home... You can count on that." She tossed the keys at me. "Guess what..."

"Drive?" I asked.

"Yup."

"I don't suppose you know where to, Aunt Shauna?"

"Actually, I know *exactly* where we're going."

Aunt Shauna had me park in the city centre, then give her the keys.

I felt I should've known better when she headed into the nearest bar and ordered two shots of tequila. Neither were for me.

"Right," she declared, leading me back outside, "if the truth won't find it's way to me, I'll find my way to the truth."

I felt my little clitty swing freely inside Gary's larger underwear, as we walked the streets.

Aunt Shauna found another bar, ordered another two shots, then led me back out into the street. "It'd be easier if you just told me the truth now, Mark."

How about, *don't call me fucking Mark!* "You know everything, Aunt Shauna."

She gave me a knowing glance.

And somehow I suspected she really did know everything.

"Don't be so arrogant-" Aunt Shauna stumbled on her heels on the cobbled street.

I caught her, then realised exactly where we were.

She straightened her back, then looked across to the Ann Summers store. "I know you were inside there on Tuesday, Mark."

I dug my fingernails into my palm.

"Do you want to tell me the truth now?"

I tried to breathe.

"Or shall we go inside and see what the staff have to say?"

My heart felt like it was having palpitations.

"Oh, Mark, you might think discretion is their middle name, but trust me I'll absolutely humiliate you if I have to."

I was sweating. I was red-faced. I felt my whole world was spinning out of control.

"So, why not just tell me the truth?"

I looked up to my aunt.

"Tell me," she said gently.

"I can't," I said finally.

Aunt Shauna took a deep breath. "Finally, we're getting somewhere." She adjusted her necklace. "You admit you have a secret... What is it?"

"Aunt Shauna, please just let me take you home. You've been drinking. Have you even remembered to take your medication?"

She raised her forefinger in front of my face. "Don't dare try to turn this around, Mark."

"Have you, though?"

She exhaled loudly. "How could I focus to remember to do anything with what I know?"

I tried to lie to myself that she still knew nothing. Not for sure.

A gentle breeze blew litter over the cobbles between us.

"I haven't taken my meds since I saw you and Gary the other day with the Ann Summers' bags."

I swallowed. "Why, Aunt Shauna?"

She hesitated.

I pondered letting it slide, in the hope she'd back down and give up. But she was my mother's sister. I knew better. "What's that got to do with anything?"

"It's everything!" she screamed in my face.

Several pedestrians looked at us as they walked past.

"Don't you understand the position you've put me in? The burden I'm carrying? I find you in town with a man old enough to be your father and *you're* the one carrying Ann Summers bags. You don't have a girlfriend. And Gary lies to me that he bought you porn movies! What truth could be worse than that if *that's* the best lie he could come up with?"

I couldn't speak.

"And, do you know the worst part, Mark?"

I shrugged.

"My gut tells me exactly what's going on... And you're too weak to stop it."

Stop it? Was she crazy? The last thing I wanted was to-

"It's written all over your face," she said finally, then turned to the Ann Summers store.

I felt frozen to the spot. I *couldn't* go in there with her. I just couldn't. I'd stood out like a sore thumb on Tuesday. I was a dead cert to be recognised today. And I knew I'd give myself away the moment I caught a glimpse of the beautiful lingerie or, worse, the glorious sex toys I longed to take inside myself. I doubted I'd even be able to deny it. Not in front of other people, and certainly not if Aunt Shauna raised her voice.

"Let's go home," she said. "You're off the hook."

"Home?" I asked.

"To *my* place. You're not going anywhere near Gary again."

I'd get to that problem later, but why wasn't she dragging me into Ann Summers as she'd threatened?

She turned me with tipsy hands and started walking me back towards the car. "It's bloody closed."

CHAPTER 38

I was sat on a chair in Aunt Shauna's house, concerned by the amount of dust my clothes were collecting.

"I bet you wish you could play with your snake," she said, plumped in the middle of – and sinking further into – her sofa.

"I beg your pardon," I said.

She held up my mobile, then shook it mockingly at me. "The game. Snake. I've seen you play it before."

"I'm not bothered."

"Liar." She poured a ridiculous amount of tequila into her glass – her fifth or sixth since we'd got here – then topped it up with a little cola. "Have one yourself."

"No, thank you, Aunt Shauna."

"What's wrong, is my tequila not good enough for you?"

I shook my head.

"I don't know why you're saying no, you're going nowhere from here until your parents are home. You *won't* be driving."

"That's okay, Aunt Shauna, I'm not much of a drinker."

"Suit yourself," she said, and downed her drink in one go.

I felt my nostrils flare, both in anger at her careless alcohol intake and at her insistence I stay. It was already Thursday evening and my parents were due home on Saturday morning. Was she really going to stop me seeing Gary before then?

Aunt Shauna started to go through my mobile.

I thought I'd deleted all previous texts between Gary and I, but I couldn't be certain.

"What d'you think'd happen...?" Aunt Shauna slurred. "If... I texted Gary, pretending to be you?"

"I think that'd be a very dishonest thing to do, Aunt Shauna, and you know that's not the way my mother and father raised me-"

"Did they raise you to go into a sex shop with an older man?"

I said nothing.

She tried to lean forward, but failed. "Are you covering something up for him, Mark, is that it?"

I looked to the patio doors, then to the living room door which led out to the hall towards the front door. I had to find a way to escape back to Gary before the day was over. Even if it meant roughing it on the bus.

"You're so readable," Aunt Shauna said, laughing. "The last bus left an hour ago, and..." She held up my mobile again. "Good luck phoning a taxi."

"He *isn't* in my house," I protested.

"Liar."

"I promise, Aunt Shauna."

She pressed several buttons on my mobile. "I bet if I text and tell him you're on your way home now, he'll reply and prove you're lying *again*."

Shit.

She accidentally dropped the phone. "Ah, hell's bells."

I tried not to squirm as I watched her try – and fail, miserably – to bring it back to herself with her foot. "Has there been any word from my parents?"

"As if you care." She poured another drink, went to down it, then stopped with the glass just beyond her lower lip. "What was I going to do there?"

I shrugged.

"There was something."

I couldn't let her remember.

"It was just a few seconds ago."

It was imperative she didn't text Gary.

Aunt Shauna pointed her forefinger at me. "This is your fault, Mark. This is what happens to me when I don't take my meds. I forget stuff."

Nothing to do with the drink then, I felt like saying. "Perhaps you *should* take them. Now, Aunt Shauna, before it gets any later... Even just one tablet."

She appeared to hold the thought for several seconds.

I watched her lose herself in her confusion. "I'll get you a tablet then, yes?"

She gestured to the mantelpiece.

I was quick to my feet to find her medication, in a box surrounded by a colony of more dust. My mother would've had a fit if she saw how her sister was living again.

"What are these for?" she asked, not moving her free hand to take the medication from me.

"Your meds, Aunt Shauna. You asked me to get them for you."

"Did I?"

"Yes."

She eyed me.

I waited for her to call me a liar again.

She snatched them from me. "Yes, and about time too." She pushed out three tablets, and shoved them into her mouth.

"Aunt Shauna, wait! That's too many!"

"Fuck off."

"You've been drinking–"

"I've to take three at a time."

"It could be dangerous–"

She downed her medication with tequila and cola.

I swiped the rest of the packet from her and returned them to the mantelpiece. I wasn't going to assist her suicide, no matter how much I wanted to go home and be with Gary.

She set her empty glass down on the sofa.

I returned to my chair.

Her eyes were closed when I looked over to her again.

I watched her for close to an hour, listening to her snore throughout, before I dared rise from my chair and creep across the floor towards my mobile.

She sounded like she almost choked for a second, but it was nothing more than a deep snort.

I reasoned she was out for the count, and grabbed my mobile. I checked quickly to see if I'd any unread texts or missed calls. There was none. No sign of any texts at all, actually.

She continued snoring.

I slipped my mobile into my back pocket. Now, where had she left her purse? I couldn't get out of here without the car keys.

Aunt Shauna went suddenly quiet.

I froze before her.

Her eyelids were moving. Almost twitching.

"Aunt Shauna?" I said aloud, fearful she was falling into a coma.

"Yes, Mark?" she said, clear as day.

"I thought you were asleep."

"Don't be fucking stupid." She forced herself to sit up. "Sorry about the language, your mother would have my guts for garters if she heard me. I tend to get a bit loose with my lips when I drink." She looked to the tequila. "Oh God, please tell me it was both of us who got through *that* much."

I shook my head.

"You sure?"

"Positive, Aunt Shauna. I don't drink much. And I've never tried tequila."

She pursed her lips. "Take my advice, don't start." She rubbed her head. "Oh God, I should take my tablets."

"No!"

Her eyes opened wide, revealing the whites to be red and bleary. "Excuse me?"

"Sorry, you've already taken three tablets."

"Three, Mark? Why the hell would you give me three?"

"I'm sorry."

She tutted. "I'll forgive you this time. But don't do that again. I could've overdosed if you weren't here."

"I am here, Aunt Shauna."

She reached out and touched my arm. "I'm glad. You can make sure I'm okay and don't do anything stupid." She handed me the bottle of tequila. "Hide this from me, would you?"

I nodded, then took it to the adjoining, open-plan kitchen and put it in a cupboard. It wasn't the world's greatest hiding place, but I knew my aunt. She'd find it if she wanted to, no matter where.

"And don't tell me where you've hid it," she said, as I sat down again.

I watched her. She seemed calmer since she'd slept.

"Mark, I'm not going to make any more wild accusations, okay?"

"Thank you, Aunt Shauna."

"But there is something I saw today I haven't brought up."

"Right."

"It was back at your house, when I walked in and found you in your Y-fronts."

I cringed.

She gazed at me for what felt like an eternity, as if even she was afraid to confront what was about to come out of her mouth.

I felt fear on an even deeper scale than before, worrying about all the implements and garments which might have been lying around the house. Was it possible she'd seen something I'd missed?

"Mark, I saw your body. There's evidence all over it that someone has struck you several times over."

Oh fuck. From when Gary had whipped me with his belt.

"You're not denying it, then?"

How could I?

"Mark, were you beaten up?"

"No."

"So, you consented to it?"

I somehow managed to keep looking her in the eye.

"Did Gary do it to you? Did you let him? Or perhaps even ask him?"

I crossed my legs in the most feminine of manners, nervously and without even thinking.

"Tell me the truth," she pleaded.

"Aunt Shauna, you heard what Madam Scarah said today... Gary's a guardian."

My aunt held my gaze, then miraculously quoted verbatim, "But not to the Mark I see."

I gulped.

"There's marks all over your body, is that what she was referring to?"

I anxiously inhaled a deep breath.

Aunt Shauna slipped back on her sofa. "Oh fuck." She steadied herself, then drew her feet up from the floor and stretched out. "What was I saying there?"

I felt a glimmer of hope.

"Oh, yes, Madam Scarah..."

I felt it extinguish.

"What a croc of shit charlatan she turned out to be!"

"Indeed," I said, feigning accompanying laughter and watching as my aunt lost the last of her lucidity.

"Get me a blanket, Mark, would you?"

I quickly retrieved a blanket from the hot press in the hall, then came back to the living room and wrapped it around my aunt, making her comfortable. "You should be out like a light soon, Aunt Shauna."

She slipped one hand out from under the blanket and touched my arm again. "You're a good kid, really..."

I smiled back to her.

"Whatever's going on."

I waited to watch my aunt pass out, then stayed by her side as she slept. She seemed safe. I reasoned it'd be okay to leave her.

I just had to find her purse.

After a few minutes of searching, I found it out in the hall on the second step of the stairs. I grabbed my car keys, gave Aunt Shauna one final check, then let myself out.

It was pitch black outside, despite it being summer.

I was late. Very late. I just hoped not too late to lose my virginity to the man I was falling-

Shut up.

I quietened my thoughts, then got into my parents' car and began to drive home.

"Gary," I called out excitedly, before I'd even shut the front door behind me. "Lover, I'm home!"

There was no answer.

I threw open the door to the living room, only to find the room in darkness.

My resolve already waning, I ran up the hall and flicked on the light in my parents' bedroom. I was horrified to find the bed empty.

The house was is complete silence.

I turned, and trudged out to the hall. Then into my bedroom.

Gary could be heard breathing quietly.

I carefully turned on the light, only to find him asleep in my bed. "Gary," I said, hoping to rouse him but also fearful of an angry response about my absence.

His deeper breathing suggested he was fast asleep.

"Gary?"

He elicited a little snore.

I stepped through the room, then undressed and left my clothes on my computer chair. I gave myself one final feel through the fabric of his underwear as I watched him. He was lying on his side, with his back to me, facing the wall. I removed his briefs and lay them next to the bed, hoping he'd wake soon and gather my scent from them.

There was only one thing for it at this hour, I resigned myself to getting caught up with the housework.

Tomorrow, though, I swore, tomorrow I'd lose my virginity to him... No matter the cost.

CHAPTER 39

I awoke on Friday morning to find Gary's underwear still on the floor. Something made me look back over my shoulder. I was taken aback when I saw him propped up on his side, staring down at me.

"Morning," he said, his voice firm.

"Morning," I replied. "Um, how long have you been awake?"

"A little while." He cast his eyes down my naked body. "I've just been watching you."

"Gary, I'm really sorry about yesterday. I couldn't help-"

He shushed me.

"Are you mad?"

He shook his head.

"Are you sure? I'd understand if you are-"

"Princess, you're so beautiful." He placed his palm on my bum and gently stroked my skin. "I heard everything your aunt said when I was hiding. There was nothing you could've done."

"I'd to wait for her to pass out on her meds before I could get away last night."

He smiled as he stroked between my buttocks.

"That's nice," I cooed. "Really nice."

Gary slid two fingers against my opening.

I nodded, encouraging him to go further.

He lay down behind me, kissed my shoulder and rotated his fingertips on my rectum.

"Mmmmmm."

He kissed my neck.

"That's so good, Gary."

He straightened his fingers. "Are you ready, Princess?"

"Yes," I said, although I wished I'd wakened first to fix my hair and apply some make-up, jewellery and sexy lingerie for him.

Gary guided his fingers into my anus.

It felt sore at first, then heavenly as my innards stretched to accommodate him.

He slipped his free arm around my chest, then pulled my back against him. He devoured my throat with his lips, then lovingly turned my mouth to his and slipped his tongue inside.

I began to gyrate my hips, making love to his digits with my rear.

He curled them inside me.

I couldn't contain my purrs of pleasure into his mouth.

He forced a third finger into me.

My ass obediently opened wider. "Gary," I gasped.

"Are you okay, baby?"

"Yes, lover." My eyes watered a little through the intensity. "It's good... Really good."

He wrapped one of his bare legs around mine, entwining us even more together. "I think you're ready."

"I am. I promise you, I am. I want this."

He licked my earlobe. "Say it, baby."

"I want you to make love to me, Gary."

He twisted his fingers inside me, feeling out the walls of my anus.

My clitty jutted out, rock hard. I found his thigh with my palm, and dug in my fingernails. "I need you inside me... I need your *cock* inside me."

Gary let his free hand roam my body, exploring my nipples first, then my navel, before taking hold of my sex. "Why the rush, baby? Let's give you more pleasure first."

My eyes rolled back in my head, as my lover masturbated my clit and picked up the pace of his fingers in my ass. "Oh, Gary, you've no idea how much I missed you yesterday... How much I longed for you to touch me like this."

He kissed the back of my neck again. "Today's your day,

Princess. I'm going to make it all about you."

I could feel his erection under my ass, poking the underside of my she-scrotum. "No, lover, it's *our* day. I want you to enjoy taking my virginity, as much as I enjoy losing it."

"Oh, I will, Princess... I'll enjoy every second."

"It'll belong to you forever," I whispered.

He squeezed my sex. "Eternity, Princess."

I groaned my way through a grunt, as he tunnelled his fingers in and out of my sphincter.

"You take hold of her," he said, releasing my sex.

As I began to touch myself, Gary moved down the bed, keeping his fingers inside me.

"Let's get you onto your back, Princess."

I was in a whirl, and needed his helping hand to manoeuvre from my side to my back. I grimaced through duel stimulations which teetered upon both agony and ecstasy. I wheezed.

"I'm going to withdraw my fingers now, are you ready?"

"Yes, Gary."

He slowly eased them out.

My whole body shook, and it felt like he was even deeper inside than was humanly possible – such was the duration of his withdrawal.

He smiled as he watched precum glitter on my sex.

I gasped, prompted by his fingertips finally fleeing my sphincter. "I feel empty already."

He reached over my body. "Not for very long, baby." He set his hand on my bedside table. "I brought this to bed with me last night." He lifted a condom. "I hoped you'd see it and wake me up."

I felt such disappointment. "I didn't see it, I swear!"

He ripped the packet open. "I know, Princess." He rubbed the head of his cock all over my tiny she-balls. "It would've been nice to have been wakened by you straddling me, though, sliding your little body down on my cock."

I had to slow my pumping of my sex. "Oh, Gary, stop it! I could cum so very easily right now."

"Slow down, baby... We have all day."

I nodded.

"You can mount me later."

I nodded profusely.

"But first..." He started to sheath his thick cock in the slick rubber. "First, I want to take you like this. On your back, legs spread wide. Oh, baby, I've imagined it from I first set eyes on you at the hotel."

"Me too, Gary." I deliberately parted my legs to either side of the bed. "Are you going to be gentle?"

An engine outside seemed louder than usual.

"I'll try, baby."

My body contorted at the possibilities his words implied, and I had to still my hand on my sex. More precum leaked out.

"You're so beautiful, Princess. I can hardly believe I'm going to make love to you."

"You are," I said. "Promise me you are."

"I promise, baby."

I watched as my lover guided his condom-covered cock under my she-balls and towards the entrance to my hole. I grabbed the bedsheet with my free hand. "This is finally going to happen!"

He looked into my eyes, then lowered his mouth to mine and kissed me as he set his cock against my rose bud opening.

I kissed him back as I felt his head pressure itself to be allowed in.

Gary stroked my hair.

My fingers tightened on the bedsheet.

There were voices exchanged outside the house.

He grunted, pushed and slowly made my innards surrender.

I gripped my sex hard as I felt my lover enter my body. "Oh my God, Gary."

The head of his cock pulsated within my rectum. "Just relax. I've got you."

I nodded breathlessly. "I want more."

He started to feed more of his gargantuan member into me.

I was delirious, ignorant to the obvious, and ascending to a physical plane I'd never been to before.

But those voices were outside my very window.

My eyes widened. I knew those voices! I knew them all too well! "Stop," I said.

"What?" Gary demanded in disbelief.

"They're here!"

"Who?"

"They're back!"

"Who, Princess? What're you talking about?"

"My parents, Gary! I can hear them outside! They're coming up to the front door!"

CHAPTER 40

Gary popped his cock from my anus.

I grimaced, momentarily, then threw myself out of bed. "Get dressed," I said, both hushed and hurriedly.

"I'll hide," he insisted, and set foot on the floor.

I spent a split-second too long gazing at his sheathed erection, then grabbed my jeans and started to pull them on. This was no time for underwear – sexy or otherwise!

The key could be heard sliding into the lock.

Gary grabbed the condom wrapper, then stuffed it into my bin.

I covered the wrapper with used tissues, as I wondered where around the house we'd left everything else. "Where'd you hide yesterday?"

The front door handle turned.

He hesitated.

"*Where*, Gary?"

"I'll prove it!" Aunt Shauna bellowed. "I'll show you both what's been going on!"

It was too late. They were already in the hall!

Gary forced my t-shirt over my head, then slapped my ass so hard he sent me careering towards my bedroom door.

"Mark, Gary, come out here!" she cried.

I stumbled down the hall.

Aunt Shauna was stood inside from the front door. We came face-to-face. She immediately tried to push past me.

"Shauna," my mother snapped, holding my father's arm on the front steps. "Help us here. Take his other arm!"

I blocked my aunt's path.

Her nostrils flared.

"Shauna!"

She reluctantly returned to the front steps, then took my father's arm.

"Thank you, Shauna," he said, his voice weak and his face pale.

"Mark," my mother said, her own voice weary.

"What're you doing here?" I asked, wet precum dribbling down the inside of my leg. "You're not due back till tomorrow?"

"*I* picked them up!" Aunt Shauna snapped. "I wanted to show them what you've been up to while they've been away!"

My heart pounded, my face was red with both rage and embarrassment, and fear encapsulated my entire body – fear my entire sexuality was on the brink of exposure. I couldn't possibly hope to hide Gary from all three of them.

"We got an earlier sailing," my mother said. "I texted you yesterday, Mark."

My eyes shot to Aunt Shauna on the front steps. "I didn't get the message."

She grinned.

"Yes, you did, Mark. You replied. You told us to have a safe trip."

I stepped back – though not aside – to let them help my father inside.

"Thanks, son," he said. "Our bags are in the car."

"I'll get them in a minute," I lied.

He eyed me with suspicion. "You're always putting off till tomorrow what you can do today, Mark."

"He's been shacked up with some middle-aged predator!" Shauna screeched.

My mother turned to her sister in the doorway, blocking her way of re-entry. "Keep your voice down. I don't want the neighbours to hear what you've been saying."

Shauna stared at her, then eventually nodded.

My mother stepped aside.

Shauna stepped in.

My mother closed the door behind her.

"Lock it," Shauna said. "Don't let them escape."

"Let who escape?" I asked.

My mother locked the front door.

"There's nobody-"

"Hello," said a voice behind me. "You must be Mark's wonderful parents."

I spun in shock to see my lover fully-clothed, smiling and extending his hand in the direction of my parents.

"I'm Gary," he said. "I was just in the shower."

All colour drained from my face.

No one accepted his offer of a handshake.

"It's him," Shauna said. "*He*'s the pervert. He's the one who's been corrupting your son, Jan. I've seen the marks-"

"Shauna, would you just let me handle this?" my mother demanded. "Please?"

Shauna's head looked like it was going to explode, but she opted to say nothing.

"Thank you."

"You must be really confused," Gary said.

My mother nodded.

My father's face looked like it was regaining some colour. Crimson. Like red mist descending on his mind. The muscles in his arms were tensing.

"What're you doing in our house and what're you doing with our son?"

My sphincter finally sealed shut.

"I've actually been staying here," Gary said.

I felt myself nearly have a fit.

"Obviously!" Shauna spat.

My mother shushed her.

"Since Monday, believe it or not."

My mother's eyes moved to mine, undressing the truth from within.

"Don't blame, Mark, please. This is all my fault. I shouldn't have asked, and he was just being kind and wonderful."

Oh God. That was twice he'd patronised them with that word.

"Tell them what you've been doing to him!" Shauna squealed.

"SHAUNA! I told you to let me deal with this." My mother slid the key to the front door between her fore and middle-finger. "I'm *dealing* with it."

I gulped. I'd seen her do this before when I was younger. It wasn't pretty.

"Go on," she said to Gary.

"There's clearly been some misunderstanding somewhere," he said.

"No misunderstanding," my mother said. "You're a stranger, stood in my house, without my permission."

"I can leave, if that would resolve the situation-"

"You're going nowhere... *Gary*."

I could see my fingers physically tremble at the sound of his name on her lips.

"Why don't you start by telling me *how* you came to be staying here? I assume this has nothing to do with a broken computer?"

"That's true," Gary said.

Never admit to my parents I lied to them! I couldn't even shoot him daggers to stop.

"I shouldn't have let Mark lie to you like that."

No, he was making it worse!

And my mother's knuckles were whitening around the key. "Then tell me why the *fuck* you made my child lie to me, Gary."

The room was shook into silence.

She'd never used language like that in her life... I thought.

"He didn't make me-"

My mother's glance was enough to silence me. "Answer me," she said to him.

He flattened his shirt on his stomach. "It's my wife-"

"Ha!" Aunt Shauna snarled. "Wife."

"She ended our marriage," he said. "I'd nowhere to go."

My mother stared him out.

He stared back.

"I don't buy it," Aunt Shauna said.

My mother kept staring.

"If his wife kicked him out, he'd have had *anywhere* else to go."

My mother kept staring, letting her sister say anything at all now.

"And look, Jan." Shauna pointed past Gary into another bedroom. "The spare bed hasn't even been slept in."

My mother finally broke her stare. She glanced to the spare room. Then she nodded. "I see that, Shauna."

"He slept on the sofa," I said, my voice little more than a quiver.

The faces of both my parents shared the same unconvinced doubt.

"He didn't sleep on the sofa," Aunt Shauna said, leaning her mouth to my mother's ear. "They're lying to you. Can't you see that?"

"Actually, that's not true," Gary said. "I didn't sleep on the sofa."

"*Where* did you sleep?" my mother asked.

All my instincts told me she already knew.

"I slept in Mark's bed."

CHAPTER 41

My heart sank. It was over. My life. My entire existence. And he didn't care in the slightest that he'd just outed me to save himself.

"And he took the sofa," Gary continued.

My mother's eyes bore into him.

"You know what young ones are like... He sat up half the night watching his movies."

My father's eyes bore into mine.

I felt such shame. I needed to go along with Gary's pretence, yet I was sure the contortions on my face gave away the imagery all over my mind – my mouth on Gary's cock... And my ass, just minutes earlier, taking him inside me.

My mother slid the key back into her palm. "Okay," she whispered.

"Okay?!?" Aunt Shauna demanded. "Are you kidding?"

My mother spun on her heel to face her sister. "Shauna, I swear to God, if you don't give it a rest, I'm going to say something I'll regret. I mean it."

"You're being a fool, Jan."

My mother stared her out.

"There's more going on here. Just *look* at the two of them. They're guilty as sin!"

I knew I had to say something before my aunt turned the tide back against us. "Mother, did Aunt Shauna tell you she dragged me to see a medium yesterday? *Against* my will."

"What?" my mother snapped, fury rippling across the contours of her face.

Aunt Shauna froze.

"Shauna, you know how I feel about those things, dabbling with the dead-"

"I can explain, Jan."

"No, you can't. They're not the dead, Shauna. They're evil spirits. I've told you to stay away from them, and now you go and force my son to go with you... HOW DARE YOU!"

"It was him," Shauna said, jabbing her finger at Gary.

"It was nothing to do with him," I said.

My mother's eyes remained transfixed on her sister. "Gary, tell me the truth, did you have anything to do with Shauna taking Mark to see a medium?"

"Absolutely nothing," he said.

"That's good enough for me."

"What?" Shauna asked in disbelief. "Jan, please. I'm your sister."

"I want you to leave, Shauna."

"Excuse me?"

"Now, Shauna."

"You're believing *them* over me?"

"Mark is my son. I believe *him*."

Shauna turned to my father. "David, do something. Please. You must see what's-"

"You heard my wife, Shauna. We'd like you to go."

Shauna's nostrils flared and her breathing heaved. She wasn't for moving. "But what about the marks all over-"

"SHAUNA, IF YOU DON'T GET OUT OF MY HOUSE, I SWEAR TO GOD, I'LL THROW YOU OUT!" my mother screamed. "Can't you see David's ill and needs his rest? We can't cope with your latest bout of mania. So, go. Whatever's going on here, I'll get to the bottom of..."

Oh shit. This *wasn't* over.

"But, right now, I just need you to go." My mother pushed my aunt aside, unlocked the front door and opened it. "Get out."

Aunt Shauna glanced from my mother to Gary, staring for seconds, then to my father and finally gave me a look of contempt. "Okay." She walked out of the house.

My mother slammed the door behind her.

My father sighed.

I stood as awkwardly as ever.

Gary remained calm and collected.

"You said you had a shower?" my mother asked, turning from the door and looking at his dry hair.

"That's right," Gary said.

She nodded. "I'm crying out for one myself. David, you get yourself straight to bed. I'll be in to check on you in a few minutes. Mark, you get our luggage from the car." She took a long, laboured breath, then started towards the kitchen. "While Mr Gary and I are going to have a little chat over a cup of coffee."

"Amen to that," Gary said.

"You heard your mother," my father said to me.

I reluctantly slipped out the front door, just in time to see Aunt Shauna speed off erratically down the street.

I trudged down towards the bottom of the driveway, believing it better to take my time and give Gary a chance to work his magic with my mother. Her instincts were usually good about people, and she'd just chosen him over her own sister. Did that mean he truly *was* a good person? I hoped so.

I found my parents' luggage dumped by the side of the road, as a million more thoughts raced through my mind.

I could still feel the phantom of Gary's throbbing cock in my anus. I shuddered. That was not the loss of virginity I'd dreamed of. It was barely a loss, awarded on a technical point if nothing else.

My mind couldn't help but wonder about my mother's conversation with Gary. How would he fair under softer, subtle scrutiny? And how genuine was my father's illness? He'd looked pretty terrible, after all, and I hadn't even asked him how he was before he headed to bed.

Fuck! Bed! My parents' bedroom!

We'd left an assortment of condoms sprawled across the floor on my mother's side!

I dragged the heavy luggage up the driveway as fast as my puny, sissy arms would permit. I left one at the bottom of the front steps, then carried the other one up to the front door.

The door opened before I got to the top step.

"Let me help you," Gary said, grinning as he easily took the suitcase from me.

"What're you doing? You're supposed to be having coffee with my mother."

"She's helping your father into bed."

Oh God. "The condoms," I mouthed, then swiftly pushed past my lover.

Lover. Ha!

I tried to walk in a combination of hurriedness and silent tiptoeing.

"MARK!" my mother yelled.

I froze in the hall.

She was stood to the right of me, alone, in the bathroom.

Which meant my father was already in the bedroom.

I leaned forward enough to see his shape under the duvet. "Yes, mother?"

"Have you brought our luggage in yet? I want to make a start on the washing."

I hesitated.

"Well?"

"Gary's just bringing the second suitcase in now," I said, hoping he'd hear me and take the hint. He was so much stronger than me, anyway. So muscular. And drop-dead, older man sexy.

"Have you no shame, child?"

I gulped.

"I raised you better than this."

Had she?

"He's your guest, Mark, go help him."

"But..." I needed to go to her bedroom.

She snapped her fingers. "Go. Now."

"It's okay, Jan," Gary called. "They're both in now."

My mother's raised eyebrows and long, exaggerated blink

said it all about how she felt about him using her first name.

"I'll stick the kettle on now," he added.

My mother shook her head. "He's really made himself at home here, hasn't he?"

I tried not to visualise all the places he'd touched me.

"Get out of my sight, Mark."

I supposed the spare room was the only room he hadn't.

"Now."

I darted, temporarily, into my bedroom, and waited. All I could hope for was that she'd leave the bathroom and head down the hall.

"*Where* are the suitcases?" she called out.

No one answered.

"Gary?" she shouted.

The kettle was already beginning to boil. He probably couldn't hear her.

Yet I heard her release an all too familiar exasperated sigh.

She stamped her heels as she hoofed her way down the hall... And into the kitchen, slamming the door shut behind her.

I didn't waste time, and leaned my head forward through the frame of my door to look in on my father.

He was lying on his side, his back to me.

I couldn't tell if he was sleeping yet, although I should've guessed by my mother's constant raised voice that that wouldn't have been possible at all. Yet I didn't wait. I walked into their room, trying to act casually – if I was caught – yet quietly – in the hope that I wasn't.

A floorboard creaked under my foot at the end of the bed.

"What're you doing?" he croaked.

I could see all the condoms on the floor. They were unmissable. And unexplainable.

"Mark?"

"Uh... I just came to see how you are."

"Fucked," he said.

I was even more shocked to hear him swear then I had been about my mother. He was more a gentleman than she was a lady.

And both *never* used bad language.

"Get out of my sight."

I looked down at the condoms. I could have them all picked up in three or four seconds. It was all I needed.

"Now."

I glanced to the bed.

My father was staring at me, with a look that suggested he wasn't too ill to spring out of bed and throw me out of the room.

I conceded a temporary defeat, and walked out to the hall. I'd wait a couple of minutes, then try again. And this time I'd avoid that dodgy floorboard.

"MARK!" my mother screeched.

Oh fuck, Gary, what had he said now. "Yes?"

She threw open the kitchen door and popped her head out. "Come here."

I went to the kitchen.

"Stand there," she instructed, and pointed right next to my lover.

I knew she knew. She hadn't found the condoms, but she knew. And now she wanted to interrogate Gary's controlled exterior, and watch my childish interiors fold to the truth.

"Go on, Gary, where you left off."

He was clutching a coffee. "Well, as you can tell by my accent, I'm obviously from another part of the country."

My mother's eyes flicked suspiciously between us both.

"Your sister said I could've gone anywhere else to stay-"

"You could've."

"We haven't lived in this part for very long."

"There's such things as hotels, Gary."

I could feel my face reddening.

"Jan, may I call you Jan?"

"You may not."

He sighed. "My wife's a very domineering woman..."

Oh God, I wondered where he'd got that inspiration from.

"... And she controls our finances."

My mother nodded.

Gary held his arms out, and accidentally brushed my chest.

I tried not to recoil, then wondered if I perhaps should've to keep the game up.

"She's left me with nothing," he said.

"And, what, that's our problem, is it?"

He shook his head.

"You can't stay here, Gary. Not only is it inappropriate, with him, but we don't know you." She made a rare, welcoming hand gesture. "You seem like a gentleman. You seem genuine. And you probably are. But, in short... You're not welcome here."

"I understand," he said.

"Mother-"

"Stay out of this, child."

"I'm twenty years old," I muttered.

Her eyes shot me into silence.

I just wanted to plead with her, *he's nowhere else to go*. Yet I knew he had. He had his real wife. His real job. His real money. And he'd be checking into a hotel in no time. Alone.

"My marriage is unfixable, I'm afraid." He held his hands up. "I'm not looking sympathy, please. I've a flight booked for tomorrow. I'll be staying with extended family at the other end of the country."

"Okay," my mother said.

"It was never my intention to be here even this long, Mrs..."

My mother leaned her head to one side, then surrendered to a half-smile. "It's okay, you can call me Jan now."

Wow.

"And, Gary, I owe you an apology on behalf of my sister. She has a lot of issues. I won't go into them."

"I wouldn't ask, Jan."

"But her behaviour was out of order. I hope she didn't embarrass you."

He shook his head.

"So, you'd nowhere to stay and my son invited you to stay here?"

"That's right," I lied.

She shushed me. "The adults are speaking, Mark."

I was so humiliated to be chastised like that in front of my lover. We were *all* adults.

"That's right," Gary said. "He really is wonderful. I don't know what I'd have done without him this week."

I looked down and realised my nipples were erect, poking through my t-shirt.

"Is your financial situation genuinely as dire as you say, Gary?" my mother asked, then sipped her coffee.

"Until we get through a divorce, yes. And that could be at least another two years away."

My mother nibbled her lower lip.

Come on, mother, I know that look.

"My relatives booked my flight over the internet," Gary said.

"And I take it you've no car to your name?"

"I have a car, Jan... Unfortunately, my wife has the keys."

My mother rolled her eyes.

I couldn't get a proper read on her.

"Listen, how are you planning to get to the airport?"

Gary reluctantly shrugged.

Jesus, even *I* was buying into his performance.

"Well, you two, I haven't had a proper look around the house yet..."

Thank God. Never mind the condoms, I'd left lingerie in the washing machine and I'd still to ask Gary what he did with the dildo.

"But it seems someone has been keeping it clean and tidy." She looked at me. "And I know that wasn't you, dear."

I beat my pride to a pulp, and said nothing.

"You *won't* be staying in Mark's bed tonight, Gary..."

I felt my face fluster. Why couldn't she have said bed*room*? I was going to give it all away with one too many blush.

"... And nobody sleeps on *my* sofa in *my* house... But, as it's only for one night, I must insist you stay in the spare bedroom."

"Really?" I asked.

Her face turned stern when she looked at me.

"Jan, honestly, I've caused too much trouble for you all already, I'll figure something else out. I'm sure my relatives will help me find a way to pay for a cheap hotel near the airport-"

"I won't hear of it, Gary," she insisted. "You're staying *here* tonight and..."

I could barely contain my excitement.

"Mark will drive you to the airport in the morning."

I'd be able to get a goodbye kiss, if nothing else!

"Jan, I can't thank you enough," Gary said, his voice sounding like his life depended on this generosity. "I don't know what to say." He looked to me. "It seems heartfelt kindness runs in this family."

My mother made her familiar fake laugh. "Take your coffee into the living room, Gary. The sun's beautiful in there at this time of day... Although you probably already know that."

My lover looked rather sheepish, as he made his way out of the kitchen.

My mother stepped across the floor to me. She lowered her voice to say, "You're not out of the woods yet, Mark. Shauna may still be onto something. And it'll take a long time for you to regain our trust."

I swallowed. "Yes, mother, I'm sorry."

"Now, get out of my sight."

I started to follow Gary's path to the living room.

"Not that way," she said. "Stay out of his company."

"Yes, mother," I said, disappointment deploying from my sphincter to my scrotum. I headed out to the hall, hoping I could finally retrieve those condoms before she saw them.

My mother walked into the hall behind me.

I panicked.

She went to her luggage. "I've so much washing to catch up with."

I hurried on towards her bedroom.

She opened the living room door. "Gary, do *you* have any washing that needs doing while I'm at it?".

I heard my father snore, and crept past him.

"OH MY GOD!"
I grabbed the condoms.
"WHAT THE HELL ARE THESE STAINS ON MY CARPET!?!"
I stuffed the condoms into my pocket.
"IS THAT BEER? MARK! GET IN HERE AND EXPLAIN!!!"

CHAPTER 42

I lay atop my bed, over the duvet, with my mind racing and my body yearning for this man under the same roof. I'd taken my mother's advice, so far, and steered clear of him, yet it was only because I knew I couldn't get a moment alone with him. I still feared giving my obvious attraction away if I'd to spend another second in his company in front of her.

When she'd summoned me to explain the stains on the carpet, she'd absolutely humiliated me in front of him, giving me the worst kind of dressing down. I explained the stains were beer I'd accidentally spilled one night, while spent on the sofa, and she berated me for drinking ale instead of a more refined beverage such as wine.

I was sure my red face was a picture.

And I could sense Gary's feelings on the subject, almost in agreement, as if beer was the last thing I should be seen drinking.

I was a sissy wine-drinker, and that was the end of it.

When she'd turned her back on me, though, I'd been able to make a face to Gary which he successfully interpreted and distracted her with conversation while I rushed outside to the garage to retrieve my lingerie from the washing machine. It appeared I now had everything successfully hidden away – toys, underwear and condoms. I didn't think there was anything I'd forgotten... Genuinely.

I lifted my mobile and wrote out a text to Gary.

ME – I'm so sorry for how today has turned out.

I waited anxiously for a reply, then got paranoid that

somehow my mother had got her hands on his phone and was already deciphering the hidden meaning behind what I was sorry for.

GARY – It couldn't be helped. Not your fault. Don't worry about it. We'll have Amsterdam next year.

I felt devastated. On two fronts. Firstly, how could I wait another year to see him again? To feel him again? To take him inside me again? And properly? Secondly, he hadn't signed his message off with any X's.

I wondered if my mother was near him. My bedroom door was shut, so I couldn't tell who was where in the house.

But I got brave regardless.

ME – I wish I could be near you xx

GARY – I'm going to the toilet in a minute. Meet me outside the bathroom.

I tried to ignore the further lack of X's, and jumped to my feet. I waited by my door. And waited.

Finally, I heard the living room door open and then close. I opened mine.

Gary came walking up the hall.

I was like a giddy, slutty schoolgirl as I gazed longingly back at him.

He smiled.

The kitchen door opened behind him.

Gary made a sharp right into the bathroom.

I came face-to-face with my mother. She had a stern look on her face.

Gary locked the bathroom door.

My mother beckoned me towards the kitchen with her finger.

Obedient as ever, I followed her.

She shut the door behind me, then stood against it, blocking my way past. "You and I are going to have a talk, young man."

I longed for the inner strength to tell her I wasn't a young man, I was a young girl and a very horny one at that, but I knew that day – if ever – was a long, long time away.

"Your father and I didn't raise you to be a liar, Mark. And you've been telling a lot of lies this last week, haven't you? I mean the broken computer, what on earth was that all about? And then more lies that it broke down again? Never mind all the others. No wonder you sent your Aunt Shauna doolally. We'll *not* be going away on holiday again. And you'll *not* be left here on your own. On the one hand, you've a good nature to let Gary stay here when he'd nowhere else to go. But you didn't tell us. That hurts. It pains us, in fact. *Why* did you not tell us?"

I hesitated.

"Do you want me to go tell Gary he has to leave now or do you want to tell me the truth?"

"No, mother, that isn't necessary."

She looked down at me. "Then tell me why you were telling lies by omission."

"I thought you'd worry, mother... And I thought you'd say no. I'd already told him he could stay-"

"How did this even happen?"

"I bumped into him," I lied. "I invited him to stay before I'd even realised what I was saying... To be honest, I didn't think he'd accept the invitation."

She nodded.

"That's the truth, I swear."

"Well, you're not to do it again. Ever. No more strangers."

I watched in agony as Gary strolled past the kitchen door and returned to the living room. "Yes, mother."

She was still nodding.

I was starting to believe I'd got away with it, and turned to walk to the door to the adjoining dining room.

"And, one more thing... If I ever find out you and that man have been intimate in this house-"

"Mother!"

"*Ever*... I will drag you to the local minister and have you undergo conversion therapy... Do I make myself clear?"

I feigned innocence. Then I said, "I'm not gay," with more convincing fervour. I wasn't, after all. I was a girl.

"Don't treat me like I'm stupid, Mark... Or I'll throw you out on the streets... Do I make myself clear?"

I surrendered to a nervous inhalation, then an anxious exhalation. "Yes, mother."

"Good, now go to your room. And *stay away* from Gary for the rest of the day. I mean it."

"Yes, mother."

"I'll bring you your dinner when it's ready."

CHAPTER 43

I couldn't believe it as the late summer evening finally turned to dusk, and I hadn't seen or spoken to Gary since our extremely brief encounter outside the bathroom – if it could even be counted as such.

My father hadn't got up for his dinner, I'd been forbidden to and I'd no idea what conversation my mother and Gary had entertained. I worried about his confidence – or, rather, overconfidence. He could be arrogant, perhaps even cocky, at times. And my mother would've been ready to pounce on any suggestion of so-called inappropriate behaviour between him and I.

But so far I hadn't been summoned for another dressing down, and he'd not texted me either.

I believed I'd heard my mother and Gary both, separately, leave the living room, use the bathroom and head to their separate bedrooms over half an hour ago.

I was so horny and unfulfilled as I lay in my bed. I so desperately needed to feel his cock again. In my palm. My mouth. And, especially, my ass.

But I knew it was impossible. My mother's ears were trained to hear every footstep upon every floorboard in our house.

My frustration was beyond belief. Gary was in the same house, and we couldn't even see each other.

I reached to my bedside table for my water, only to find the glass empty.

I kicked my pyjama-clad legs out of bed, and quietly made my way to my bedroom door. I gently opened it to find my parents' bedroom door wide open. Mother was obviously intent on listening out for me doing just exactly what I was doing.

My father snored, heavily.

And then I noticed something else. So was my mother. Perhaps overly tired from all their travelling.

I journeyed on with soft steps and made my way to the kitchen, carefully opening the door to avoid any squeaks from the hinges, then I shut it behind me. I placed my glass under the tap and filled it up again. I was just about to take a swig when I heard the door open again behind me.

He quietly closed it behind him, then just stood there, gazing at me.

I stared lustfully back over my shoulder at him, in only his white boxer shorts.

He surveyed my tight ass in my pyjamas.

I reasoned if I stayed at this side of the room and he remained at the door, we couldn't be wrongly accused of doing anything my parents wouldn't approve of.

"We need to talk, Princess," he whispered, then pointed to the dining room.

I instantaneously abandoned my need for caution and adopted the obedience he'd instilled in me, creeping across the floor to the dining room.

Gary followed closely behind.

I yearned for him to graze my rear with his fingertips, but he didn't.

He shut the door tight behind him.

I set my glass down on the table on a coaster – my mother would've killed me if I'd forgotten to use a coaster – and stood beside the wall, out of sight of anyone who might appear in the kitchen. "I'm so sorry about today," I whispered.

Gary was stood by the glass door, in sight of anyone, but able to keep look-out. "Me too," he replied. "It's been very disappointing."

I looked down, ashamed.

He reached his hand out and lifted my chin. "Hey, it's not your fault."

I found myself instinctively rubbing my chin against his fingertips.

"I've so much sympathy for you, Princess."

My heart was beating fast, knowing we could be caught together at any moment. "Gary, you've no idea how good it is to hear you call me that again."

"You'll always be my Princess."

I mustered a smile.

"You warned me how controlling they were, but I genuinely couldn't believe it until I saw it for myself."

"Elaine said it too."

He grinned.

"What?"

"I was just thinking about your mother chastising you for drinking beer instead of wine. It's more feminine, after all."

"Gary, do you think she knows?"

"Knows what?"

"About me? About what I am? *Who* I am?"

He thought for a second. "Subconsciously, she's probably always known... But she fights it... And I can't tell you if she'll ever accept it."

I sighed.

"Maybe she'd come 'round quicker if you met someone closer to your own age," he said.

I pressed my fingertips into my heart. "I don't want anyone younger, Gary. I want you. I've totally fallen for you... I'm besotted."

His eyes strayed to the door.

"Is someone there?" I asked.

He shook his head.

With only the light from the kitchen to illuminate us, I pulled Gary away from the glass door and out of sight. I stared at his lips, then pressed mine to his for a kiss.

He kept his mouth closed.

I burned for more, and tried to slip my tongue through.

Gary resisted.

My fingers found the outline of his bulge through his boxers.

He quietly grunted, his breath escaping his lips into my mouth.

My tongue found a way through the gap.

He returned the most wonderful of embraces, swishing my tongue around his, as his cock grew with my touch.

I tried to pull at the waistband of his boxers.

Gary broke the kiss and held my wrists back from his body. "Princess, we can't do this here. Not now. You've too much to lose."

"There's only one thing I care about losing, Gary, and you know what it is."

He sighed, his thumbs stroking the skin of my arms.

I gently moved my fingers to my pyjamas, then dropped them to my ankles to reveal the lace front of my g-string.

"Wow," Gary whispered.

"Touch me," I said. "Touch *her*."

He brought his fingertips to the lace wrapped around my clitty, then slowly stroked.

"Mmmmm."

His hand felt incredible on the almost see-through fabric.

I grabbed his bulge again, squeezing it.

His eyes widened. "I didn't intend for this to happen when I got up, Princess."

"When you followed me." I smiled, teasingly, then pulled his cock over the top of his boxers. "I thought I was going to have to wait a year to see this again." I touched his foreskin, slowly rolling it back in my palm. I gripped it harder, forcing it to stiffen. I was so determined to make sure I got what I wanted this time.

Gary flicked his fingers around the tiny circumference of my clitty.

I felt every manly inch of his cock in my little palm.

He kissed me again, coating my lips in his saliva.

My heart pounded and heat rose swiftly within, knowing my parents were under the same roof and suspicion about Gary and

I was rife.

He pulled my body suddenly against him, kissed me more deeply and dwarfed my crotch with the sheer mammothness of his own.

I threw my arms around his muscular upper body and let my fingernails fray his back. I knew the dangers, but the risk was only emphasising my need for reward.

Gary pulled my hair, arching my back, and devoured both my neck and shoulder with his teeth.

I dragged my fingernails lustfully through his flesh.

His naked cock throbbed against my lower abdomen.

I had to have it, and reached between us to hold it again. The warmth was so welcoming. Alluring, in fact, and so much so I need to feel it against the bare skin of my own sex. I swept my panties to one side, exposing my clit, then grazed Gary's cock against her. I groaned as we made contact.

He continued to kiss my skin, concentrating between my throat and neck, and pawed at the cheeks of my rear.

I yearned to feel him between them, as I rubbed his member over my little clitty. "I love how much bigger you are," I whispered.

"Because you're my girl," he replied, then licked my lobe, stimulating another erogenous zone he'd introduced me to.

I slapped my sex with his.

Gary broke the kiss.

I slapped it again.

He watched.

A third time, I whacked my little clitty with his shaft, then massaged his bulging balls beneath. I looked up to him. "I have a condom in my pyjama pocket."

He looked over his shoulder to the kitchen, then back to me. "What're you waiting for, Princess?"

I kneeled down to retrieve it, saw his cock right in front of me and engorged it with my mouth. Oh my God, it felt incredible! I couldn't control myself. I sucked it fastidiously, taking it to the base within the first several sucks.

He ran his fingers through my hair.

I gagged, then suppressed my need to cough.

Gary started to slip it out.

I threw my face on it again, and sucked my man's member down towards my throat.

He quietly groaned in the dark.

My ears constantly scanned the silence of the night for one creak of a floorboard out of place. I knew it'd take something to drag me away from this cock now, but unfortunately my mother really was something.

Gary's balls hung loose on my chin.

I pulled him by his rear against me, pinning the back of my head against the edge of the dining table.

My man knew exactly how to handle my most desperate of desires, and mercilessly pounded my mouth.

I jerked my tiny clit below.

He drilled deeply into me, jamming his balls against my face.

I tried to slurp at his shaft to no avail, such was the ferocity of his force.

Gary wrapped my hair around his fingers, so he could propel my head back and forth at his will.

I knew it was stupid to surrender so much control, given the magnitude of risk – I was unable to hear every sound I should've been listening out for – but I was a slave to servitude. And nothing made me happier than when my own needs were outstripped by the demonic demonstrations of his.

Gary's grunts were still subdued, but they were escalating.

I recklessly pummelled my little clitty in my palm. Saliva drooled from the corners of my lips to my top. His precum too.

I had the condom wrapper in my free hand and started to slide it up Gary's leg to his thigh.

He snatched it from me.

I momentarily gasped – for air – as he pulled his gigantic prick from my mouth. I looked up to him.

He stared down, a devil in his glance, then he pulled my little frame to my feet with just one hand. "Are you sure about this?"

he asked.

I stilled my hand on my clitty. "Yes."

"I need to hear you say what you want, Princess."

My eyes darted to the door to the kitchen, then back to his. "I want you to take my virginity, lover."

He removed my hand from my sex. "Say more."

"I want you to make love to me, Gary."

He leaned his forehead to mine, his chest still puffing as he panted over me. "More... Say it like you really mean it, sissy."

I gulped.

The house was silent but for our intense breathing.

"Sir, I want you to fuck me like a whore."

He hauled me around by my elbow, bent me over and shoved my face onto the table. "Your funeral," he muttered.

CHAPTER 44

He ripped the wrapper off the condom, then tossed it onto the table.

I tried to grab it, planning to stuff it into my pyjama bottoms.

Gary seized my arm, pinned it behind my back and held me still in place. "Don't move, you sissy slut."

"Gary, you have to let me hide that. If my parents-"

He slapped his huge cock across both my buttocks, stinging me into silence. "Good girl... Obedient when most required."

My eyes transfixed on the condom wrapper. I couldn't just leave it there. If we heard a single sound, we'd have to break apart, I'd have to pull up my pyjamas-

Gary hauled my g-string down to my ankles. He sheathed his shaft behind me. "You better pray no one gets up," he whispered, then placed my palms on my cheeks, urging me to hold them open for him. "Because wild horses aren't gonna stop me once I get started."

I felt the beat of my heart ricochet off the wood of the table back to my chest. "Please, just be quiet."

He began to rub the head of his cock around the outer ridges of my hole.

My sphincter involuntarily shrivelled.

He pushed himself against my hole.

I tried to prise my prize open.

Gary groaned in frustration, momentarily abandoned his effort, then spat on his shaft and rubbed in his saliva. "Just relax, baby. You already know you can take it."

I couldn't relax. Reality was quickly beginning to overrule my desire for insane, late-night, forbidden sex with my lover. My parents were probably 25-30 feet away, separated by three walls and two closed doors. If I believed they couldn't hear me, then how the hell would I ever hear them when Gary started to-

He slid his bulbous head into my ring.

I wheezed out an uncontrolled breath, breaking my hands from behind my back and covering my mouth.

He held himself an inch or so inside my entrance for several seconds, as he tenderly stroked my skin, encouraging me to relax.

I gently tried to push my rear backwards onto him.

He met my effort with a huge stroke of his own.

I clamped my lips shut as my ass suddenly cocooned Gary's entire cock.

Gary moaned quietly. "You have the most perfect, little ass pussy, Princess."

I couldn't believe it. I could actually feel his lower abdomen against my buttocks. I'd really taken him all the way inside in one go. "Mmmph," I mumbled through the cracks between my fingers, as perspiration from my palm mixed with my saliva.

He leaned his upper body over my back, brushed my hair from the side of my face and kissed my ear. "This is only going to be a slow fuck for your first time, baby," he said.

I nodded my understanding – and my gratitude.

"Next year in Amsterdam, you'll truly learn what it feels like to be a whore." He grabbed the condom wrapper from the table and stuffed it into his boxers. "A souvenir."

I felt him throb through every part of my rectum.

He kissed my cheek and met my gaze. "Ready?"

With my eyes wide with fear, I reluctantly whispered, "yes," through the tiniest gap in my fingers.

"You mean the world to me, Princess."

I watched the warmth in his eyes shine, then fade as he withdrew his member back through my love tunnel. I suppressed all sounds and retreated in thought, as the sensations drove weakness into my knees.

My lover paused at my entrance, his last couple of inches

remaining inside me, then started to slide all the way back in again.

I felt my innards struggle, as if the instinct of innocence was to resist such penetration, and the beginnings of cramp itch in my bowels.

Gary's subtle groans inspired me.

I found satisfaction in knowing I could take such a grand cock so deep in my so-called ass pussy, and hoped pleasure would soon follow.

He kissed the nape of my neck momentarily, then slid more quickly backwards. He volleyed himself forward again, at a swifter pace.

Pre-cum from my clitty kissed the wooden edge of the table.

"I know I have to, baby," he said quietly in my ear, "but I don't want to rush."

I somehow willed myself to squeeze my canal around his cock.

Gary responded, tunnelling himself in and out of me, and left his torso leaning over my back so he could shower my neck in his soft, tender kisses.

I was gently eased from an agonising brutality to a fiendishly beautiful plane of pleasure, feeling loved, adored and cherished. I tried to motion my rear to meet his strokes, but my body was mostly pinned down in subservience. I cared little to protest. I was made to be debauched by this incredible man.

He powered his shaft along the walls of my rectum, his pace at once reckless and ordained. His lips peeled back on my flesh, and his teeth sank in.

I mummified my wails in my palm, seconds later succumbing to the wonders of embracing such lustful pain.

Gary retreated his fangs, then tongued my wounded skin as if he could somehow miraculously heal it.

My erect clitty became trapped between the table and my lower abdomen.

His enduring pace, propelled pleasure to her as friction played its part.

My eyeballs rolled and a joy-fuelled exhalation escaped through my fingers.

His mammoth balls slapped both my lower buttocks and the top of my thighs.

I could no longer focus on the sounds of the house. I was a prisoner to our lovemaking. To our lustful bodies entwined as one. To the hope that this monumental act between us would make him see his future lay not with his wife, but with-

"Princess," he said in my ear, as his grunts escalated.

I tried to stretch my mouth to his. I wanted his kiss. I needed it. But I couldn't reach. I couldn't give him that final act of coercion.

He forcefully held down my tiny arms.

My sphincter stretched so far around him that pain returned over pleasure. But as my heart pounded and my sex danced against the table, I realised the aphrodisiac of intensity. I sacrificed my selfishness to it, and embraced the agony over everything else. Including my safety. I no longer felt myself at home. I existed only against my lover's body. And hoped he existed only inside mine. I forgot all about the risk we were taking. That *I* was taking. I hadn't a thought for my future, or the consequences.

"I'm close," he whispered.

I'd relive this act for the rest of my life.

"I don't want to cum yet..."

Wonder what I could have done differently.

"But I can't slow down."

Wonder what I *should* have done differently.

"I can't stop."

Wonder what might have been.

Gary's solid steel-like shaft tore deeper inside my rectum. His snarls in my ear escalated. His grips on my arms tightened. His teeth clamped again on my skin.

I whimpered.

He pounded my behind like a monster.

I believed I was experiencing the closest to perfection I ever would.

He was possessed by his devotion.

I was wrong.

His lust.

Delightfully so wrong.

His love, I wished.

I sensed his cock change within me. Imagined his balls tightening, as they so often did. And found the strength to fling my booty upwards, to make my hips meet his and heighten his arousal.

He bit into my neck.

I wailed silently into my hands.

Gary raised himself over my body, and powered down into my asshole with one final, almighty stroke.

I was pinned to the table, my little clitty squashed and somehow squelching.

Gary erupted gargantuan globs of spunk into the condom, steeling his orgasmic need to roar through gritted teeth on my flesh.

I must've cried. My eyes watered. Pain engulfed my anus, arms and neck. My wetness coated the dining room table.

Gary collapsed on top of me, yet still his cock ejaculated more and more.

My ass pussy truly drained his spectacular balls.

His grunts turned to groans.

I let my fingers slide open across my mouth.

"Baby?" he asked.

"Sir?" I whispered.

"You're shaking... Are you okay?"

I knew he couldn't see it, but I was smiling.

"Princess?"

I could barely believe it myself, but I had to tell him, "I came... I came without being touched."

His cock throbbed inside me. "Show me," he said, and pulled me with up with him as he stood.

We gazed down together on my orgasm, languishing across

my mother's beloved dining room table.

"I hope it doesn't stain the wood," I said quietly, trying not to giggle.

He stroked my arms. "Don't let it then. Lick it up. All of it."

I shook my head, then twisted my neck to look in his eyes. "No, Gary, I want you to do it."

"Me?"

"Yes, quickly. We've come this far without being caught. Eat up my cum. I want to know there's a part of me inside you."

Gary hesitated.

I kissed his lips.

His eyes were locked on mine. "*All* of it?"

I smiled. "Yes, daddy."

He mouthed, "Daddy?"

I kissed his lips again. "Do it for me, if you really care."

Without warning, Gary hauled his hard on out of my hole.

I gasped, the sudden withdrawal almost paralysing, and grabbed the side of the table for support.

Gary went down on one knee.

I watched him survey my love juice glistening in the light from the kitchen. "Don't think about it. Just do it. Eat me."

Gary threw his mouth to the table.

My eyes lit up with wonder.

He hungrily feasted on my deposits, kissing, tonguing and then loudly suckling on them.

I couldn't resist toying on my softening clit.

Gary noticed, and reached out to seize her. He pulled me towards him. "You too," he said.

I bent over to join him, and licked my she-sperm up from the table.

He rubbed my rear. "You're always going to be mine now."

I swallowed my cum down deep, then, with some still lingering on my lips, I asked him, "Do you promise?"

Gary stood up straight.

I watched as he carefully peeled the condom from his cock, ensuring he spilt none of the phenomenal volume of contents.

"Mmmmm," I whispered. "You're going to make me swallow every last drop, aren't you?"

"No, Princess." He guided me forward by my little clitty. "Keep her hard." Gary placed the condom over the tip, then sheathed my entire sex in the latex rubber.

I couldn't believe the sensations as my clit was bathed in his sperm.

He sealed it around the base. "Don't spill any."

It turned out to be one of the most shocking, yet arousing, moments of my life. "I won't, sir."

He crouched down to collect my g-string and pyjama bottoms, then pulled them up my body. He stretched my underwear high, sealing my sex safely in his condom. "You're going to sleep in that."

I could barely breathe as I nodded. His spunk was so warm. I could feel it around every part of my clitty.

He tucked his cock back into his boxer shorts. "We should go to bed now."

"We've been so lucky so far, Gary." I smiled. "I can't believe I'm not a virgin anymore."

He wrapped his palm around the outline of my sex, then squeezed, squelching her in his semen.

I felt it in my heart in that very moment. I loved this man. I'd do anything for him... And *anything* to be with him. Permanently.

He let go of me before I dared tell him. "Night, baby. I'll go first."

I grabbed his wrist as he turned to leave. "Wait." I dragged his mouth to mine.

Gary passionately kissed me.

My she-penis pulsated. My sphincter parted. I wanted him inside me again.

He broke the kiss. "You're gonna get fucked like that every night in Amsterdam."

I went weak at the knees.

"Goodnight, goddess."

I watched as he turned, opened the door to the kitchen and crept quietly through the house. As I waited for the quiet sound of him closing his bedroom door, my mind centred on one devastating thought – how was I going to make it through the next twelve months, waiting for him to make love to me again?

CHAPTER 45

I awoke in the morning a mucky mess. A beautiful mess of Gary's making. My entire crotch and much of my lower abdomen were saturated in his sperm.

I slid my palm around my erect clitty and made a fist with his condom in between. I groaned as I began to masturbate, knowing he was only a couple of rooms away and imagining he was able to join me. How I craved his touch. Wished for his hard cock in my mouth. And fantasised about taking fingers, toys and more in my tight, little ass pussy-

"Mark!" she bellowed. "Gary's already awake. It's time for you to get up and take him to the airport, like you promised."

My fingers were frozen around my sex under the duvet. "Yes, mother," I said quietly.

She watched me as she waited. "Hurry up then."

"I will." I just needed her to leave the room first.

"I'm waiting, Mark."

I sighed loudly, hoping she'd take the hint.

She didn't budge.

My pyjama bottoms – and my g-string – were around my ankles, and it was as if she knew and relished the prospect of catching me in the act.

Now *she* sighed loudly.

My pulse quickened – and I felt it even in the pulsations of my she-penis through my palm – as I remembered several times in my younger teenage years when she'd been equally suspicious of my activities and pulled the duvet from me. That'd been then. This was now. I'd never be able to explain the cum-filled condom on my-

"Wakey, wakey, sleeping beauty," Gary chimed in, appearing alongside her and looking handsome as hell as he stared down at me.

"I'm awake," I whispered, my face now burning red.

He had a gaze of lust on his face. "Well?"

Join me, I died to implore him.

"Get out of bed, Mark," my mother said firmly.

"How's dad?"

"I'm a good lot better," my father answered, sticking his head around the door frame. "But you have to get up, son. Your good friend Gary here needs a lift to the airport."

I lay still.

"Get up *now*, Mark," my mother said. "Stop delaying."

I gulped.

Her eyes widened. Her stance changed. She was about to make a grab for my duvet.

"Jan," my father said, reaching his hand out to hers. "Come on. Let's grab a quick coffee in the kitchen. Leave these two be."

Leave us be? Leave me and knowingly let me get dressed in front of the man my mother had already voiced suspicions about me being intimate with?

"Jan."

She ignored him.

"Jan."

Her eyes were like furies in the night sky as she stared into me.

"Jan."

"Yes, David! All right!"

I watched with a glint in my eye as she retreated, defeated, in the wake of her husband, and listened to their footsteps funnel all the way down the hall and into the kitchen until the door was shut behind them.

"Morning, beautiful," Gary said quietly.

"Get down here and kiss me," I whispered, beckoning my lover to me.

He came to my bed, took my head in his hands and slipped

his tongue into my mouth.

My sex ached to release my love juices into his semen.

Gary kissed me with more fervour than expected, as he peeled the duvet back from my body.

I was breathless when he broke away.

He looked down at me. "Wow, Princess, even when you're a mess you're incredible." He took my hand away from my clitty and replaced it with his own. He started to masturbate me in silence, switching his gaze from my groin to my eyes and back again.

I tried to take the immeasurable pleasure in silence.

The kettle could be heard beginning to boil in the kitchen.

He thrust his hand flawlessly up and down my erect she-shaft.

I met his strokes with faster ones of my own, feeling his sperm saturate my she-skin.

He watched me yearn for another kiss, yet denied me all the same.

My pyjamas and g-string were still around my ankles, as was my duvet.

The kettle was louder than ever.

I knew it was possible for someone to sneak back up the hall. To walk in us. To catch us now after everything we'd been through together.

"Cum," he mouthed.

I nodded, as some of his semen slid out from the condom and ran down my scrotum.

"Obey me."

"Yes, sir," I said, and fucked his hand for all my worth.

He throttled my clitty in return.

My growing pants were increasingly more difficult to suppress.

Gary slid his free hand into my top and tweaked my nipple.

I felt my tiny, little she-testes start to seize.

He tweaked the other.

The sound of the kettle faded away.

CHAPTER 46

I started to turn left at the bottom of my street.

Gary looked back over his shoulder. "I have to say, Princess, I'm gonna miss that place. Your parents' bungalow sure is in a nice neighbourhood..."

I felt my heart breaking inside.

"A beautiful neighbourhood," he added. "You're a lucky girl."

I burst into tears.

"Hey, hey." He placed his palm on my knee. "What's wrong?"

I struggled to drive on, wiping my cheeks with the back of one hand. But the tears kept flowing.

"Do you want me to drive?"

I nodded, then pulled the car over to the side of the main road. "I don't want you to go, Gary."

He sighed.

"No, I mean it. I *really* don't want you to go. How am I supposed to go on from here without you?"

"Baby, you'll find a way."

I didn't care that we were in broad daylight in my own neighbourhood, as I took hold of his hand on my leg. "You've made such a difference to my life, Gary. I know who I am now. For sure, with no doubts. I don't want to go back to living as a male. I don't want these baggy clothes. I want the lingerie-"

"You can have that-"

"I want the sexy day clothes, the condom filled with your cum I've still got sealed around my clit and... I want you, the man of my dreams, to spend those days with."

He sighed again.

"What, Gary? Don't you want the same things?"

"Of course, Princess. I'd love to be with you every day, but I live hundreds of miles away. I have a job, a life, a family."

More tears spilled from my face to my top.

He reached to wipe them for me. "We'll see each other again, I promise."

"In Amsterdam?" I snapped. "In a year? I don't know how I can wait that long. I'll go insane, Gary, trapped in this body without you here to make love to it."

He glanced to the clock above the radio.

"Yes, your flight." I unfastened my seat belt. "Let's swap seats then."

Gary drove out of the city in silence, headed for the motorway to the airport.

The dampness between my legs was doing nothing to ease my suffering.

"How are you now?" he asked finally.

My sobs had ceased several minutes earlier. "I don't want you to laugh at me, Gary."

He planted his free fingers between my closed thighs, but in a tender rather than an erotic manner. "I promise I've no intention of laughing at you, baby."

"I don't want you to think I'm just feeling this way because I'm young, or silly... Or inexperienced."

He gently stroked the skin of my legs through the fabric. "Princess, I'm beyond proud that I've been a part of every one of your experiences this last week."

I struggled with the lump in my throat.

"Try to think of the positives. There's so many of them."

All I could think was that this man I'd let first into my head, then my body and now my heart was going to be leaving me in a matter of minutes.

"Princess, you said it yourself, you have a new understanding of yourself. You know, without doubt, who you are and who you wish to be-"

"And who I wish to be with," I interrupted.

He sighed. "You have new underwear. You'll find your moments alone to dress up. You can wear them under your day clothes."

I pulled my baggy top up to reveal my bra.

"See, baby?" he said, his voice full of joy. "You're already doing it."

I wondered how much he was looking forward to seeing his wife again after a week. There was no mistaking the difference in our demeanours.

"You have those toys too, don't forget. You can have a lot of fun on your own, act out a lot of your fantasies-"

"*Our* fantasies, Gary."

"Yes, Princess... And you now have a proper friend in Elaine, who you can be herself around. Trust me, you'll be glad of her in the months to come."

I felt myself beginning to weep again. "But I won't have you."

"You will. I promise you. We can e-mail, we can text, we can even talk on the phone. We'll get through this. We *will* be seeing each other again."

I wanted to ask him if his wife ever took any trips away, but I couldn't face the answer my instincts already told me.

"I'll pay for Amsterdam, baby. I like you *that* much. All you have to do is make sure you turn up."

"Gary, I'd turn up anywhere in the world to be with you tomorrow, if that's all you asked."

His eyes remained fixed on the motorway. "I can't ask anything of you, Princess. You understand that."

I felt my insides churn as we passed another sign for the airport. We were getting so close.

"Princess, haven't you ever thought about having a boyfriend your own age?"

"No," I said firmly. "It'd be impossible with my parents being the way they are."

"What if your parents weren't an issue then? Wouldn't you like to meet someone your own age? Someone free to spend everyday with you?"

"I don't know... Maybe... I used to think about it. But I wouldn't want anyone else now I've found you, Gary. I mean that. You've no idea how deeply I feel about you."

He sighed.

I knew I had to tell him the truth. I had to say those words. Every look of stress on his face when I gave him the answers he didn't want to hear told me this was about to be the end if I didn't. But I had to try. I had to.

"I have to be realistic with you, Princess. Someday, you may want more than what I can give you."

Yesterday had been that day.

"I have a wife I have to go back to."

And today was the day I had to make him see that he didn't have to go back.

"I hope if you ever do meet someone else that you'll feel you can tell me about it... About him." Gary cleared his throat. "I won't be mad. I understand you're twenty-seven years younger than me... And you're single."

"I don't feel single, Gary," I whispered. "Not anymore. Not when I'm around you."

He said nothing.

I couldn't find the words to say anything more.

A sign for the airport read 1 mile.

Gary eased the car into the drop-off zone outside the airport, parking it next to the sliding doors at the entrance.

I wouldn't even be able to watch him leave for more than a few seconds.

"This is my stop," he said, almost apologetically, as he switched off the engine and left the key in the ignition. "Will you be okay to drive home?"

I felt like shaking my head. "I'll have to be."

He reached out to brush my long hair away from my face. "Hey, don't be like that. We *will* see each other again. This isn't the end, Princess."

I turned my face into his fingers, longing to kiss them.

I looked to his eyes, then his mouth. I longed to kiss him everywhere.

"I know," he said. "I want to kiss you too."

I was shaking as I got the words out of my mouth, "Take me with you, Gary."

"What? How? Where would you stay?"

"Leave your wife. Gary, be with me. We could be happy together. I know I could make you happy... *Happier* than you've ever been."

He gazed into my eyes for the longest time, but he hesitated somewhere between breaths when it seemed he was finally going to say something I needed to hear.

I grabbed his hands in mine. "Gary, we could live together. I could live as your new wife. I promise I'd do things to you every day she never could. And do all those housewife chores you already know I can. I'd make sure you wanted for nothing."

He looked up to my forehead, then down to my lips. He smiled as he returned his gaze to my eyes. "You *are* amazing, you know that. You'd make me very happy."

"Yes, yes I would!"

"But, as I've already explained several times before, I have a family and I've no intention of breaking that family up."

"Your kids are grown up, Gary. They've left home. You wouldn't be breaking a family up."

"I would," he said, as if reluctantly.

I knew he wanted the same things I wanted.

"If I broke their mother's heart, they'd never forgive me-"

"You wouldn't have to tell them about me, Gary. I promise. I'd stay hidden. I've already lived my life hidden. I wouldn't care, as long as I lived with you. I want to be yours so much, you've no idea."

"Princess, please-"

"I love you, Gary," I said, holding back the tears.

His eyes roamed to my mouth again.

"I'm *in* love with you."

He looked up to my eyes.

I willed him to tell me the same. To turn my hands over. To take them firmly in his. And to lead me into the airport with him.

He said nothing back.

I broke down again, as he withdrew his hands from mine and unfastened his seatbelt.

He opened the driver's side door and started to get out.

I unfastened my belt, then jumped out of the passenger side. I didn't care who saw my tears. I couldn't hide them. And I had to hold him one last time.

He came around to my side with his luggage.

The doors of the entrance slid open beside us as other passengers made their way inside.

"Hug me," I said.

Gary didn't hesitate. He threw his stronger arms around me and pulled me into the tightest embrace.

I couldn't kiss him. Not in public. Not here. Not back then in 2001.

He rubbed my back with his beautiful hands.

"I'll wait for you," I said in his ear. "I promise you I'll wait." I'd wait for that wife of his to die, so we could properly be together.

He nuzzled the soft skin of my cheek with his stubble. "I have to go now."

"I know." I was whimpering.

He began to break the hug.

I wouldn't let him, and held on tighter.

"I'll miss my flight, if you don't let me go," he said.

"I accept your terms, Gary."

He didn't laugh out loud.

But I felt his slightest giggle against my body.

And then he broke the embrace and lifted his luggage. "I'll see you next year in Amsterdam."

I couldn't speak. I felt like I was choking.

Gary hesitated for a moment.

Silence hung in the open air between us.

He turned towards the entrance, then walked through the

sliding doors.

They shut behind him.

My lover was gone.

I stood alongside my car, then felt the most cruellest of ironies as his condom slid from my clit and fell down the inside of my leg.

EPILOGUE

My drive home seemed to take forever, traffic zooming by me on the motorway as I swiped tears from my face every few seconds. When the lanes finally converged, and the road led into the city, I felt mentally exhausted as well as physically fatigued.

I was broken.

My only place to go was home, yet it was the last place I felt I belonged.

I drove out of the city, shed the last of my tears for now and navigated my way into my home town.

How different these roads felt now without Gary by my side.

I indicated right, and turned up into my street.

I saw the bungalow up ahead in the *beautiful neighbourhood*. No part of this place felt beautiful anymore.

I turned into the driveway, then glanced across to Jim and Betty's house, half-expecting to see her half-hiding behind one of her curtains, checking to see if I was alone or with the handsome, older man I'd been hanging around with all week. There was no sign of her.

I stopped the car in front of the garage, switched off the engine and applied the handbrake.

I looked up to my bedroom window. That room – that bed, especially – would feel emptier now than ever.

The garage door jolted suddenly, then began to slide upwards.

I reluctantly stepped out of my parents' car.

My mother stood in the garage, staring coldly back at me.

I looked to what she was holding between her fingers, and froze.

The car had been parked over it for days. That was why I hadn't noticed it. How I'd forgotten all about it. Until now.

"What's this?" she snapped.

I stared defiantly back at her.

"Answer me, now!"

"That, mother," I began slowly and confidently, "is my fucking ribbon."

TO BE CONTINUED IN
2002: AN ADVENTURE
IN AMSTERDAM